THE CONTROLLER

LINDA COLES

Blue Banana

All rights reserved. This book or any portion thereof may not be reproduced or used in any manner whatsoever without the express written permission of the publisher except for the use of brief quotations in a book review. This is a work of fiction. Names, characters, places, brands, media, and incidents are either the product of the author's imagination or are used fictitiously. Any resemblance to actual events or persons, living or dead, is entirely coincidental.

Copyright © 2017 Blue Banana

Published by Blue Banana

Chapter One

THE WHIR of the drone's engine sounded like a giant bumblebee approaching in the sky above. It circled the park several times, observing who and what was there, anything that piqued The Controller's interest, before veering off in the direction of leafy suburban streets and back gardens. Those who heard it looked up searching, pointing, and wondering what it was doing. What was it watching? Was it Big Brother? Or was it someone else, someone with an agenda all their own, someone looking for something specific and quite probably up to no good. Human reaction was always the same, The Controller mused. No one ever thought it was Amazon delivering a book to some lucky person or a takeaway being delivered by a technology-savvy nearby restaurant. No, drones were always a thing to be curious about.

The drone picked up height and flew back out over the huge evergreen trees to a street several rows further behind. This street was a little more upmarket than the last, houses with big back gardens, conservatories, a place where the more wealthy folks lived. The Controller could hear the whir getting further away but from his control pad he could see exactly where he was and it didn't take long to spot a prospective target. He let the drone hover while he studied it. There, walking along the road, was a pretty blonde, with her little treasure walking along beside her. He watched to see which house she went into and made a note of it on his phone app, adding it to the other addresses he'd found over recent weeks. This one looked a little more promising than the last one, and after Niles had given him a bollocking last night for bottom feeding rather than going for someone with a higher value, he was happy with his find. He clicked 'active track' on his screen and watched the drone take over, following its target and avoiding nearby trees and power poles like it had eyes in its head, which it did, five to be precise. When he'd watched her go into the house, he made a mental note to himself to come back tomorrow and double check the location, that she wasn't visiting a friend and she did actually live there, just to be thorough; there was no room for mistakes.

The Controller was an important member of the group; he was the one responsible for finding the right targets and getting the details right. Being such an important cog made him feel good, and wanted. They couldn't do their job quite as well without him at the controls, though Niles, the group's self-imposed leader, would never admit that he was extremely talented at it. Niles reckoned they were each easily replaceable but Pete was anxious to fit in and keep working with them. All his life he'd been a bit of an outcast, a geek, someone who was more comfortable sitting in his room surfing the web or playing games than out with his friends socializing. He had no real friends at school and never got invited to kids' parties, and that hadn't changed through his teens either, a stint in Juvenile Detention not exactly helping, so he'd stayed in his room by default. Then he'd met Niles and Vic, and the group gave him a purpose, he had a role to fulfill as The Controller, and that made him feel like he had a place in the world, though he wished he could be as forward-thinking and in control as Niles.

Still, he was happy with his lot – for now. And he loved this part they gave him, to be in control if only for a short time, out choosing targets. They knew they couldn't really do without him and the drone and the other techy stuff he could do, so they let him tag along, gave him a place in their operation and he was grateful. And the money wasn't bad.

Focusing his attention back on the little screen, he brought the drone back to the park and, before it ran out of battery life, circled round one more time to check for any other possible targets. Today he'd found a good one. Niles would be pleased. But they may as well do the other one too, the one Niles had complained about, the one he'd found yesterday, the old lady. Why discriminate? Her money was as good as anyone's, wasn't it? She'd had her own little treasure with her and he saw no point in ignoring the opportunity.

The powerful drone came back in to land by his feet where he stood in a quiet spot just along from the park entrance, and he quickly put it in his backpack. Folks were always suspicious of someone with a drone, and he didn't want to cause himself a problem, so he hurriedly packed his gear away and set off back to his car to phone in and give Niles and Vic the news on what he'd found. He was sure they would be pleased with him.

Chapter Two

GEMMA LOVED GOING out with Pam and stood patiently waiting as Pam locked the back door, then they set off to the park together. Gemma knew the route by now, they'd been doing it almost every day for the past six years, and she obediently walked beside Pam until they got to the park gate, at which point Pam would bend down and remove her leash, letting Gemma run around and stretch her legs. Every evening, rain or shine, would be the same and Gemma loved it, it was the highlight of her day. Pam let her go as usual and slowly walked alone on the pathway as Gemma charged off into the distance, bobbing in and out of trees and scaring birds off the grass. There were always a few dog walkers in the park at this hour and she knew many by face. She'd never stopped to chat with them but they were on nodding terms, with just a couple of exceptions. A couple of the older folks were happy to stop and chat, usually when Pam sat for a rest on a bench, but more often than not, they kept themselves to themselves and continued moving. Gemma's silky golden coat shone brightly in the evening sunshine as she raced back, panting and out of breath. With bright eyes, pleading eyes, Gemma looked at Pam for the ball.

"Oh all right then, there's no hiding it from you, is there?" Pam said laughing, and she threw the small green tennis ball as far as she could, watching it bounce a couple of times before Gemma was able to pounce on it and bring it back home. Pam knew the routine just like Gemma did – and as Gemma returned back at her feet, again dropping the ball from her mouth like it was a prize, Pam took it and threw away, Gemma chasing off after it. This usually lasted about 10 throws, by which time Pam had usually had enough exertion for her older body. On the last ball return home, she clipped Gemma's lead back on and walked the nearly exhausted dog back towards home, just a few streets away. The sun was gone now, and twilight was settling in nicely and it was cooling down. In another month or so the evenings would be heavy with the summer's heat, lingering like a warm fog, clinging to your skin and keeping you from sleep. Pam didn't dislike summer, but found the hot days and too hot nights hard to bear, keeping comfort from her. She turned up her road, the birds busy getting ready for bed in the trees above her head as they walked back, their singing so loud it was almost deafening at this hour. The thought of birds jostling for branch space above made Pam smile. She bent down and petted Gemma on her shoulder, the dog looking up at her with happiness twinkling in her eyes, love written all over her face.

"Nearly there now, and I'll get you a fresh bowl of cold water, how does that sound?" As she rose back up, Pam could see what looked to be a woman coming down her front path in the near distance, a younger woman, someone she didn't recognize.

"That's odd, Gemma, I wonder who that is?" she said quietly, wondering if she'd better call out before the woman left. As they neared her gate she did so.

"Excuse me, are you looking for me? Only that's my house." The woman turned, a little startled, Pam thought, but it was hard to tell in the twilight.

"Oh, sorry. No, I was looking for Aunt Lilly's house and I went in the wrong gate. Sorry to have bothered you." Then she walked off, rather hastily Pam thought. Something didn't feel quite right. Aunt Lilly? There were no 'Lillys' in this street, and as she watched the young woman get into her car, she thought that even more odd. Surely if she was going to her aunt's, and had realized she was at the wrong house, she'd then go to the right one? It made no sense to get in her car. The small green car drove off down the road with the woman at the wheel and Pam stared after it for a moment. A light breeze blew and Pam shivered in her light cardigan.

"Come on then, Gemma, let's get you some water." Pam couldn't help wondering if she'd just come back in the nick of time.

Chapter Three

THE NEXT MORNING Pam rose and let Gemma out into the back garden as usual, then flicked the kettle on for her first cup of English Breakfast of the day. She stood looking out of the kitchen window, at the riot of colour that filled her postage-stamp-sized lot. She didn't mind that it was so small, it was just enough for her to keep up, and the colours made her happy. There was every variety of bedding plant you might find in your local garden centre, with no thought to colour grouping or co-ordination whatsoever. A space was found for it somewhere. It was chaos. The light sound of wind chimes outside on the porch tinkled in through the open door, and the early-morning sun was starting to warm the back of the house, like a warm blanket wrapping round on a cold day. She often sat outside on the porch, on the swing seat built for two, but Gemma was the only one that shared it with her now, Graeme having been gone for six years. They'd been a happy couple, together almost since school, childhood sweethearts but he had been tragically taken one day with a massive heart attack while he was out at work, one that he never stood a chance of surviving. That's when she'd got

Gemma. She missed Graeme dearly, but Gemma helped to fill the void he had left, in her house and in her heart.

The click of the kettle switch pulled her out of her reverie and she poured the hot water onto the single tea bag. She gave it one stir with a spoon to set it on its way to brewing, something her mother and her mother's mother had done, although they'd done it with loose tea back then. "Tea bags are the sweepings up off the tea floor" her mother used to say when bags first came out. But still, a single stir then leave it, that was the way to a good cup. Gemma padded back indoors, toenails clicking on the lino her own morning ritual complete though not as complex as Pam's, and flopped on the floor with a giant sigh.

"Too hot already, Gemma? And it's not even fully summer yet. Perhaps we should look at getting your coat clipped a bit?" Gemma just looked up, confusion in her eyes, then slumped back down again.

"I'm off to work in a wee while, so you'll be on your own until lunchtime when I get back, okay?" Gemma knew this to be so, Pam told her the same thing each and every workday morning, and she grew to ignore it, as dogs do. Pam added milk to her cup, threw the tea bag in the compost bin under the sink and took her tea out onto the porch where she sat and surveyed her riotous garden. Large overly stuffed terracotta pots filled in for the lack of vacant flowerbed space, every corner of the garden was crammed with colour, and the hanging baskets off the porch roof framed the whole scene like a colourful frill on a postage stamp.

"Shower in five minutes, Gemma, and tonight we should do some dead-heading, those geraniums are beginning to look messy. And we should really do something about that verbena before it gets out of hand, it's gone like a triffid." Pam talked to Gemma all the time, largely because she had no one else in the house to talk to, and she knew Gemma was listening and appreciated being included in important decisions like which plants needed dead heading first. So she carried on and didn't care if anyone heard her and thought she was losing her marbles – let them try living on their own.

The little carriage clock on the porch window ledge chimed 7.30am and said she needed to get a move on, so she tipped the dregs of her morning tea into a nearby garden pot and went indoors to get ready. At 8am on the dot she left her little house at the end of a quiet road, Gemma safe on the swing she'd herself not long ago left, and walked the couple of streets over to the school where she worked, like she did most days. In another few months she'd be retiring, but the thought of giving up her job altogether wasn't a pleasant one, she'd have to do something with her time. Maybe some voluntary work or private tuition, she wondered. Had she been a little more alert that morning, she would have seen a little green car, a car that had been parked nearby just the previous night in the dusk, a young woman at the wheel, watching her leave.

Chapter Four

As Pam entered her front gate at lunchtime, she instantly knew something was wrong. There was no happy bark coming from the backyard, no Gemma vocally greeting her as usual.

"That's odd," she said out loud to herself. "Gemma!" she called a little louder, "I'm home." Nothing. Not a sound as she walked through the house to the backyard, only the gentle tick tock of the carriage clock in the porch. Pam tossed her bag down and went straight to the back door, expecting to see Gemma fast asleep in her bed on the porch. As she opened the door, her heart sank – the bed was empty, there was no sign of Gemma. Standing there for a moment, taking in what she was – or was not – seeing, she wondered if perhaps June next door had her, maybe something had happened and she'd taken her in? Leaving her house, she made her way down the back garden path to the little adjoining gate Graeme had once put in some years back, so the two women could get into each other's gardens easily.

"Gemma!" she called, expecting to see her in her friend's yard, but again, no sound.

THE CONTROLLER

"Hello Pam," said June, coming to her own back door and walking down the little path towards her, drying her hands on her apron as she went. She wore a dress in a lavender print, and Pam would normally have commented how pretty it was. Today she had other things on her mind.

"Hi June, have you got Gemma by any chance? She's not home."

"No I don't, sorry. That's odd, that she's not at home."

"Yes it is, and now I'm starting to worry, where can she be? She's always here, never been one for getting out. I just thought maybe you had her, maybe something had happened." Her voice was filled with worry and June felt sorry for her friend, putting her arm around her shoulders.

"Listen, come on in, I'll make some tea and we'll make a list of all the possible places she could be." She steered her friend back towards the house and indoors. Though June hadn't seen anything, she herself couldn't help wondering what could have possibly happened to such a loving and well-behaved dog. She wasn't the type to get up to mischief.

Thirty minutes later they had a list and Pam was feeling a little better, though still worried, and it was almost time to get back to work.

"I'll call on these while you go back to work, and the moment I find her I'll let you know, okay?" June was a good sort, they'd been neighbours for the last 15 years, and as June knew Gemma well, Pam agreed to her plan, although she knew she wouldn't be able to concentrate at work for the afternoon. But she had to return, and knew June would be true to her word.

By 4pm when Pam got back home, there was no good news message from June and still no sign of her little dog. Pam was getting increasingly panicked. But what could she do apart from go out and search for her herself? She grabbed Gemma's leash and set off for the park, calling Gemma's name as she went, but there was simply no sign of her and no one had seen her. By 7pm Pam had to call it a night, she was exhausted both physically and emotionally, and realised the only thing left for it was to call the police. Her dog, she was sure, had been stolen.

Chapter Five

"REALLY? YOU CAN'T DO ANYTHING?" Pam was trying to reason with the desk sergeant, who was just doing his job, but which was of no help in finding her beloved dog.

"I'd like to say we can help you madam, but a lost dog simply isn't a police matter. She's probably managed to get out, gone off on an adventure and will be home before you get your cocoa," he said smiling. While his eyes and smile were kind, it wasn't helping Pam in the slightest.

"So you won't help me then?" Pam sounded dejected and she knew it but it was how she felt.

"Look, all I can do is file a report and suggest you contact the pound, the RSPCA and other shelters and see if anyone has handed her in. It happens all the time. And if she's microchipped, any vet that comes across her will notify you directly. So fingers crossed eh, safe return by the morning." His friendly smile was still missing what she actually needed – help in finding her best friend. She had no choice now but to go home, it was getting late and the mental fatigue was hitting her hard, as were as her poor feet.

As she left the station she wondered what else she could

possibly do. June had already rung the pound and animal shelters. By now Pam was sure Gemma hadn't just nipped out of her own free will. Something or someone had happened in their quiet cul-de-sac during the morning, but she'd no clue as to what that was. She only hoped Gemma would come to no harm.

Back home, Pam sat slumped at the little kitchen table, brushing out an imaginary crease in the cloth for something to do. She'd called everyone she knew to see if anyone had seen her, but she already knew the answer, nobody had seen a thing. It was like Gemma had simply vanished. The last thing she thought of giving a try was to post something on the local online community page, The Daisy Chain. Letting people know online meant more people would be aware that Gemma had gone missing and could look out for her, so she pulled the page up on her iPad and quickly scanned the last few posts. Nothing about anyone finding a Spaniel, but plenty about graffiti and petty theft. She left her own post:

From @litlady – "Can you please keep your eyes open for my Gemma? Golden Springer Spaniel, missing from Sunnymead Road this morning. Out of character for her and I miss her terribly. Please share with your friends and help bring her home."

Pam didn't leave her telephone number, not on a public site, but she did add a recent photograph of her pet. All she could do now was keep searching and wait for any comments of news and hope that someone had already taken her in while they found her rightful home. Though she was desperately tired, she knew she'd never sleep a wink tonight. She was right.

Chapter Six

THE PRETTY BLONDE wasn't paying anyone any attention, and that was just as well. He'd watched her before, had already singled her out, and today he was double-checking the facts he already knew. She'd only be in her late 20s, Pete thought, with bouncy blonde hair that he'd like to run his fingers through on another day. He wondered if it smelled of Pears shampoo, like his mother's did when he was a young boy, before his dad had gone and beat her to death in a drunken frenzy one night. The man was still inside and would be for some considerable years to come.

Now, as a 19-year-old man, Pete had left the system and was making his way in the world on his own, working scams with Vic and Niles – not exactly what he'd dreamed of as a lad but it brought money in. Back then he'd wanted to write books, become a famous author like Dickens or Child or Rowling. He saw them as all the same – as people really good at their craft. His mum used to tease him about his books – he always had his nose stuck in one, an adventure moving around in his head like a play being played out for only him to see. He wondered as he watched the pretty blonde if she liked to read, and what she did with her days. After all, if she wasn't at work at this time of the morning, or the time he saw her yesterday, she must be a young housewife or something like that, because why else wouldn't she be at work?

He took the drone out of its backpack and began its set-up. If this pretty blonde was going to be their next target, he needed to confirm where she lived and that the white toy poodle was actually hers. Using his small screen as the control pad he set things in motion. The propellers started to turn and whir and he launched the drone into the air, a bird's-eye view on the screen in front of him. This thing could fly up to 400 feet high, well out of earshot of most people, but he wanted detail so he usually flew at 50 or 100, which was about right, and if he kept it back a bit most people didn't know it was there. And today, neither did she.

The toy poodle trotted obediently alongside her and as the drone followed them back along their upper-class street to their house The Controller once again felt pleased with his find. All the houses up on The Heath were massive, with huge green leafy gardens and well-to-do neighbours, nobody short of a bob or two. Investment bankers and the like bought a home there, those well off that commuted to London, to the City each day and had expensive long lunches with clients and celebrities. Nah, she could afford it all right, or more likely her husband could, and since he got a cut of the money, he thought they should charge this one more. It was the same risk whoever they dealt with, so the upper echelons should pay more to balance out those lower down the food chain. Like the old lady. And it made up for the odd one that fell through – it wasn't often their scam went wrong, but it had. Last time, they'd had to move town rather quicker than they'd planned on, and that was always inconvenient, and costly.

He watched his screen as she unlocked and entered the

front door of her huge red brick house and went inside – again. Yes, she definitely lived here and that white poodle was definitely her beloved dog. Let's hope she loved it a lot. He called the drone back to base and, after putting it away, headed back to his car to call the details through to the others. Niles would handle the rest from here.

Chapter Seven

THE FOLLOWING morning there was still no sign of Pam's beloved Gemma. Pam made herself a pot of tea as usual and gazed outside to the empty garden, where normally Gemma would be going about her own routine but today it was sadly empty. With a heavy heart she slotted a single piece of bread into the toaster. She'd missed dinner last night, the deep empty feeling in the pit of her stomach making her too sick to eat anything, and she doubted that a single slice of toast was going to be any easier. As she'd laid in her bed last night listening for any sounds of Gemma's return, she'd decided that she wouldn't be going in to work today and instead would spend her time searching the streets and parks and asking folks if they had seen her. She couldn't just sit around hoping, she had to do something. The toaster popped and the sound returned her thoughts to having to eat something. She smeared butter and strawberry jam on the slice, trying to make it more palatable, and sat out on the porch to eat it. June popped her head over the garden fence, two large pink curlers visible on the top of her head.

THE CONTROLLER

"Still no sign I see?" June herself looked forlorn at Gemma's disappearance.

"No June, nothing. I barely slept a wink last night listening for her coming home, I'd so hoped she'd wander back in as though nothing had happened." June could see the anguish the little dog's absence was causing her friend but didn't know what to do or say, everything seemed so pointless.

"You going in to work today?"

"No, I'll let them know in a minute. I'm going out to look again."

"Well I'm coming with you, two sets of eyes are better than one and we'll cover more ground. What time are you heading out?"

"When I've got dressed, so say thirty minutes?"

"You've got it. I'd better get my skates on then myself. Toodle!" June always made Pam smile when she said 'toodle', it was part of her sunny personality, but not today, though she was extremely grateful to her friend for the help and for the company. Last night searching on her own had worn her spirits out, not just her feet.

Thirty minutes later, both June and Pam were making their way into the village centre when Pam spotted Ruth coming towards them on the pavement. She stopped to say hello.

"Morning Ruth, how are you?" Pam asked, not quite as jovial as she usually was, she sounded flat to her own ears. She had taught Ruth a good 10 years ago when Ruth had been a student in her English Literature class, and still saw her occasionally when she visited her father and step-mother who also lived in the village, though Ruth herself now lived in South Croydon. Ruth was also the founder and administrator of the online community site The Daisy Chain, something she'd

19

started up some months back to help solve community problems and raise awareness of petty crimes for people to be watchful of. An avid crossword doer, she loved a good local conundrum though she hated some of the issues that arose, particularly the more serious ones. They'd had things like the underwear snatcher, petty thieves, a missing person, and now a missing dog. The missing person had been found safe soon after their disappearance and Ruth hoped the same for her Gemma.

"Hello Pam, I'm good thanks. I saw the post about Gemma last night on The Daisy Chain, any news yet?"

"I'm afraid not Ruth, no. And no comments from anyone seeing her either, I checked before I came out. I can't think where she's gone, only that someone has taken her." She stopped and remembered her manners. "Sorry Ruth, how rude of me, this is June, my neighbour, she's helping me look for her." The two women exchanged pleasantries and Ruth gave her attention back to Pam, who was visibly upset at the whole thing. Pam continued, "And the police say it's not for them, no evidence she's been taken, but it's so unlike her, it's all I can think has happened to her, someone's got her." Tears started to well in Pam's eyes and she fought to control them but they spilled down her cheeks in thin wet streaks. June passed her a tissue and put her thin cardigan-covered arm around her friend's shoulders in comfort.

"Look Pam, I'm not sure what else I can do but I'll keep an eye out and re-post your message again later today to make sure as many people see it as possible. Let's hope it stirs something up, and whoever may have her returns her, and soon." Pam smiled weakly at Ruth and thanked her for her concern, though Ruth wished she could have done more.

"Well I hope you get lucky today and find her, let me know if I can do anything else, and keep me posted when she comes home." Ruth could only be positive outwardly, though inside she felt less sure, but didn't say anything. She watched as Pam and June slowly strolled on together, noting that Pam looked tired out already and it was still early on in the day. She crossed her fingers for the dog's safe return.

Chapter Eight

❧

Pam was resting in her chair in the lounge all by herself – the day had almost been too much for her. If she'd retired last year instead of hanging on, Gemma would never have been left on her own and would still be here now. Instead, she was missing and Pam's spirit was as flat the carpet she walked on, but when the shrill ring of her telephone in the hall called out, she bolted out of her chair, saying a quick prayer, hoping that it was good news, that someone had found her. In a way it was.

"Hello, Pam speaking," she said breathlessly.

"Listen carefully. Consider this a ransom call. We have your dog." The male voice was curt and direct in its approach and as rough as an emery board in its sound. Pam took a moment to take the words in, let them circle around and compute inside her head before she realised what exactly the voice was telling her. She openly gasped out loud, her blood chilling in her veins.

"Oh my lord."

"I see I have your attention now. If you want to see your dog alive again, here's what you'll do."

"Yes. I'm listening, please, tell me." Her trembling voice gave away just how worried and scared she was. She had no control over her emotions and the thought of some stranger with Gemma made her head spin. As she listened to the man through the receiver, she could hear a faint barking in the background. Was that her? Was that her Gemma? She struggled to listen for more but she couldn't be sure, it was too far away.

"Tomorrow night, the park where you walk her each day, bring £500 in an envelope, put it in a Sainsbury's carrier bag and drop it all in the bin by the seat in the middle of the park. Then head for the bench by the water fountain after the drop and if you've done exactly as I've asked, you'll find her. You'll be watched. If you call the police or we see them about, she's gone. Understand? 6pm on the dot." Then the line went dead, he didn't wait for an answer.

Pam stood frozen still in the hallway, the receiver still in her hand, the dial tone replacing the rough voice that was there only moments ago. Her legs gave way and she fell to the floor – the thought of some heartless stranger holding Gemma for ransom, was all too much on top of the strain and worry of the last couple of days. She closed her eyes and slipped into darkness.

"Pam! Pam! Come on love, Pam, wake up." She could hear the sound of June's voice but she couldn't answer, and was vaguely aware she was lying on the floor but couldn't understand where or why. Slowly, her eyes fluttered open and she regained her senses, one at a time.

"Oh Pam, there you are! Thank god, what happened? Are you hurt?"

Pam took a moment to collect her thoughts and

remember what had happened. But when was that? How long had she been out?

"What time is it?"

"What? It's just gone 8pm, why?"

She'd been out a while. She struggled to sit up. June gave her friend a hand and helped her to her chair in the lounge where she flopped down, exhaustion emanating from every pore. June waited for her to speak and wasn't expecting what she finally said.

"Someone's got Gemma. They have her."

"Who? Who's got her, what do you mean?"

"A man called, he has her. He wants money, tomorrow." She turned to her best friend before adding, "June, it's a ransom demand, they want £500 for her safe return tomorrow night."

"Holy hell. A ransom eh? We must tell the police."

"No!" Pam shouted. "No, they said I'd never see her again if I told the police. I can't risk it, June, I have to pay them, but I don't have that much. What will I do?" Fresh tears started to roll down her face once more, her eyes still red and puffy from lack of sleep and worry. Pam's distress was evident and June felt so sorry for her friend.

"How much short are you?"

"I have £300 in the bank, that's all until payday."

"No matter, I have the rest. What are the instructions?"

Pam filled June in on what they demanded and the more she told her friend, the better she began to feel – it was all coming to an end, like a bad dream. At least Gemma was alive, that's all that mattered.

"Excellent Pam, we can do that. Look at it this way, by this time tomorrow night, Gemma will be safely back here with you. We'll do as they say, drop the money and bring her home." She smiled at her friend to give her hope and was encouraged to see her visibly relax a little. June changed the subject, her voice concerned.

"I'm betting you haven't had anything to eat again eh? That's why you collapsed. I'm going to make you a sandwich, you need to keep your strength up, or you'll be no good tomorrow night," and left the room to go to the kitchen and make it for her. Pam stayed in her chair, the stress really too much for her, her body feeling like a dead weight. But at least she now knew when Gemma would be home; it was just one more night without her.

Chapter Nine

"Come on Bubbles, let's go." Lorna could hear her dog yap at the prospect of going outside and watched, smiling, as she came bounding down the hallway ready. The little white poodle never needed to be asked twice. Lorna stood with her leash, ready to attach it before they headed out and on to the park.

"Walkies first then I've errands to run, you want to come?" She gave her a scratch behind the ears as she spoke. Bubbles' ears pricked up in doggy response to something that sounded far better than lazing around the back garden all day.

As usual at this time in the morning, they entered the park and, after one quick check around from Lorna that no big dogs were nearby, she let Bubbles off her leash. The little poodle took off like a rocket and Lorna marvelled at just how fast her legs could go for the size of her. Lorna followed behind at a distance, watching her dog fly in and out of the bushes, sniffing round fence posts and the bottom of trees, thoroughly enjoying herself.

"Bubbles!" she called, and from a bush to her right the dog sprang out like a jack-in-a-box. Lorna took the rubber ball out

THE CONTROLLER

of her pocket and tossed it her way. The games began, with Lorna, like most dog walkers, taking and throwing the ball and their charge retrieving it. That's all dogs wanted, wasn't it? For you to just throw the ball? Want a treat? Throw the ball. Want a scratch? Throw the ball. Want some water? Throw the ball. The thought amused her, the dog was happy as long as she threw the ball. After fifteen minutes she'd had enough and they both stopped to drink from the water fountain.

"It's going to be a warm one today, Bubbles," she said to her dog, who was sitting by her feet for a moment. "I'm going to sit here for a few minutes, so go and play then we'll go off and do our errands." The little dog looked up at her, ears pricked, and she trotted off towards the shade of the bushes, her tongue hanging out of her mouth, panting hard. Lorna watched her wander off and sniff around then sat back to enjoy the warm sun on her face, closing her eyes. Ten minutes later she was ready to go and called Bubbles. But the dog didn't return.

Lorna called and called, but she never came back. She asked other dog walkers if they'd seen her that morning but no one had, and the longer she shouted, the more concerned she got. After an hour and a half of searching and calling, she decided to head back home in the hope Bubbles had got bored and had made her way back on her own.

"Yes, that's what's happened, she's waiting for me at home, poor thing must be too hot." She said it out loud so she could hear the affirmation and it made her feel better, the volume adding a sense of certainty. She wasn't thinking about what she'd do if the dog wasn't there. She picked up her walking pace and hurried back towards The Heath, scanning gardens and side roads as she walked, expecting to see the white ball of curly wool peeing up a tree base where she shouldn't be.

By the time she got to her own front door, she was extremely worried. Bubbles wasn't there. And what was she going to tell the family if she didn't come back? She decided to go back out and have another look after lunch, figuring Bubbles was probably hiding someplace like the mischievous dog she was, and she would eventually wander home when she got bored of waiting for Lorna to finally find her. She hoped.

Chapter Ten

PAM HAD to go in to work the following morning. The school relied on her to deliver lessons for waiting students and not stay at home waiting for her dog, no matter how valuable she was to her, nor how worried she was. She'd had to fib yesterday to cover her absence, something that really went against her grain, and told them she'd had a migraine. She couldn't have done the same again though she wished she could. Today, tonight actually, she would get her beloved friend back and she couldn't wait, wait nor concentrate. One thing this whole episode had galvanised was that she was finally going to retire, and never leave Gemma again. She glanced around the room, her students' heads all bent as they worked on their essays, and she was glad of the quietness this classroom brought.

She glanced at her wristwatch; it was nearly 2pm, only four more hours to go. Her mind kept wandering off to what would happen later that evening. She'd got the money ready as asked for, all wrapped neatly in a Sainsbury's carrier bag, and she knew which bin to drop it in. Since the man with a sandpaper voice had not called back again, she assumed

Gemma would somehow appear or be returned, though never having been in a ransom situation before, she was only guessing. In movies, someone always seemed to escort the captive person at a switch-over point on a deserted road someplace, but this was a small village south of London not the Bronx or rural Germany, and Gemma was a dog.

The shrill of the bell sounded that the class was over and dragged her attention back to what she was supposed to be doing, so she quickly shouted instructions to her students as they hurriedly packed their books back into their bags, no doubt glad that the boredom of English Lit was over for another week.

"And don't forget to read the next chapter before our lesson next week, we'll be discussing it then so it's important!" she shouted above the din, though suspected all ears at this point were deaf. When the final student had left the room, she stole a glance at her phone and the screensaver of Gemma.

"It won't be long now my love, and I've got you a lovely bone as a welcome home treat. Soon you'll be back where you belong, hold on a little while longer." With a heavy heart, she put her phone away as the next class noisily spilled in through her door.

At 5.45pm Pam set off towards the park, the money almost burning a hole in her handbag, which was strung over her shoulder satchel-style. She thought that if these dognappers were okay about stealing dogs, they were probably okay about stealing handbags too, particularly those they knew contained £500.

Pam walked through the park, taking a good look around. She'd listened to their words of warning and not gone to the police. Only June knew about the ransom call, so there were no officers lurking in bushes waiting to pounce, though she really wished there were. If they'd done this to her, they'd undoubtedly done it to others in the past and probably had plans to keep their scam going as long as they could get away with it. The thought made her heart feel heavy. Up ahead, Pam could see the rubbish bin for the drop. She knew exactly where the water fountain bench was, though from where she was, she couldn't see it yet. The park was quite busy at this hour, which she guessed was part of their plan, to blend in with a dog and go unnoticed.

Pam checked her watch again as she walked. It was time, so she got the little plastic-covered envelope out ready to make the drop, and with one last glance around, put the whole package into the designated bin then carried on walking. With all her heart she hoped they kept their side of the bargain. On shaky legs she carried on towards the water fountain, not daring to look back in case she saw them and they changed their minds. The last couple of days had taken their toll on her physically and mentally and her whole being felt jaded. She wouldn't wish the anguish and misery she'd gone through recently on her worst enemy. Then she heard a familiar yap up ahead. Trying to focus her ears, she wasn't sure if she was imagining it or not but as she got closer to the fountain, there in the distance, tied to the bench, was a familiar golden sight.

"Gemma! Oh Gemma!" she shouted, tears busting through her tired eyes and rolling down her face as she somehow found the energy to jog over to her little dog. She bent down to make a fuss of her, laughing as Gemma yapped and Pam untied her, both delighted to see one another again.

"Oh, Gemma, I've missed you so much! You've no idea quite how much. I'm never leaving you ever again. Thank goodness you're back!" The words tumbled out as fast as her tears of joy flowed, Gemma yapping and jumping all over her, and Pam enjoying every second of the attention. "Come on, let's get you home, I've got a nice big bone waiting for you,

you'd like that, wouldn't you? Yes you would, my love," she said in that cutesy voice people talked fondly to their pets in. Gathering her leash, a bright smile back on her face and a heavy weight off her shoulders, they both turned back headed for home.

Had Pam been paying more attention to her surroundings, she would have seen a familiar woman walking by in the other direction, but she went unnoticed, just as the woman had known she would be.

Chapter Eleven

LORNA COULDN'T UNDERSTAND where Bubbles had vanished to. It seemed she had been there one minute and gone the next, and as time had progressed she'd become increasingly concerned. She'd told the children Bubbles was at the beauty salon and staying overnight and, as they were only four and five years old, that had sufficed. For now. She'd told her husband the truth, that Bubbles had seemed to vanish, but he'd assured her the dog would wander back on her own, and went back to reading his newspaper. Lorna, wasn't so sure.

Now, as she walked through the park searching for Bubbles again, calling her name, Lorna felt sick to her stomach that something had happened to her. The park was quite busy at nearly 6pm, the early summer sun still warm as she walked, and she let her mind wander along with her eyes. She noticed someone on the swings, it was a young woman, just sitting there, but the odd thing was, she had no child with her. Why would a grown woman be hanging around at the swings without a little one in tow? She put the thought to the back of her head and carried on, up the concrete pathway, on her usual circuit, a circuit she would normally walk with

Bubbles. Birds sang in the trees as she walked, a light breeze blowing her wispy blonde hair into her face and she pushed it away. Further on she saw an older woman put something in the rubbish bin as she passed by then watched her move on, towards the water fountain, wondering where she'd seen her before. She looked familiar and seemed a little anxious but Lorna had nothing apart from intuition to base that feeling on. Maybe she was a regular dog walker too, and she had seen her in the park perhaps, though if that was the case, where was her dog now? Lorna carried on her search, calling and checking in the larger shrubs and bushes as she went until she reached the perimeter of the park, then turned back to go home, without Bubbles. She felt sad and deflated. What was she going to tell the children if Bubbles didn't come back tomorrow, she couldn't be at the beauty salon forever. Visions of Bubbles jumped into her mind and raced around in no particular order: the day they first brought her home, the day she'd been sick and spent the night at the vet, the first time they'd taken her to the beach at Brighton and she'd been delighted with the waves, and how she snored softly when she lay in front of the open fire in the lounge in winter. What the hell was she going to do? She made her way back down the park pathway and that's when she noticed, by the water fountain, the older woman again, the one she thought had seemed anxious earlier, but this time she did have a dog with her, a Springer Spaniel. What struck her as odd now was how much of a fuss the woman was making of it, like she was greeting a long lost friend again, talking animatedly to it, the little dog yapping with delight. At least someone was happy this evening, she thought, and picked up her pace towards home, passing the swings again, the woman sitting there earlier now gone. And so it seemed was Bubbles.

Chapter Twelve

"This cow can afford it, so let's ask for a whole lot more."

"Come on Niles, let's not get greedy here, we're doing all right as we are, aren't we? Isn't double enough?"

Vic was generally the voice of reason and when Niles and Vic were having a disagreement, Pete kept out of it. While Pete was with the rest of the group, he knew his place, and that was back to being Pete instead of The Controller, the bottom of the pecking order. Both Niles and Vic had a volatile side, he'd seen what happened when Niles got angry, he still had the scar to prove it from where he split his top lip after thumping him in the mouth last year. And Vic was no different, though she kept her fists to herself. But when the two of them riled each other up, it was best to keep your head down and let them mouth it out between them. Like now. Pete had given Niles the address of the pretty blonde as well as the phone number to place the ransom call, but because she lived in a fancy area, he figured she could pay double.

"Nah, I'm asking for £4000 this time, make up for the little old lady that Dufus over there snagged us," he said, pointing at Pete with a stumpy middle finger. "Not a lot of use was she? £500 smackers is sod all worth it. Whatever the figure we ask, it's the same amount of risk, so the minimum is now a grand. Bear that in mind now would you when you find the targets." Niles had a smoker's mouth, fine lines across his top lip, spittle gathered in the corners. Pete had the good sense to nod his agreement as a reply and went back to his laptop. Whatever.

"Right then, a grand it is, but I'm warning you Niles, getting greedy could backfire and we'll either end up having to dispose of a damn dog or having to leave here if things get too hot too quickly." Vic the voice of reason again. They'd not long moved into the area anyway, their last patch over at West Ham hadn't proved itself as a lucrative area at all, all tight arses Niles had said, and he was probably right. And Vic didn't like hanging around on her own as lookout either so they'd split and found Caterham and the surrounding well-to-do 'burbs.

"Yeah I got that, Vic, I hear you. Let's leave it at that. I'll make the call tonight and she can get the dough in the morning. We'll do the drop at lunchtime, no need to wait with this one, lazy cow doesn't work for a living anyway, she'll be home poncing around all day." It wasn't lost on Pete that Niles had never worked a full day in his entire life. But he stayed quiet, why risk it?

"Right," Niles announced as he looked at his watch. "It's 10 o'clock now so I'll ring her now, then who's coming down the pub for a swift one. This money is burning a hole in my underpants."

"Yes, okay, let's do this then go, you coming, Pete?"

"Yeah, I'm coming," he said half-heartedly, not really wanting to but feeling like he should. If he wanted to keep in with these two, he'd better make an effort, because what else would he be doing?

THE CONTROLLER

"Then we'll meet you down there then Niles, I'll get the first round in," said Vic, and the two of them set off for the pub, leaving Niles to make the next ransom call. Pete had given him a post-it note, the words 'white poodle' and the number, no name, so he dialled it. He waited, and waited some more, listening to it ring out at the other end. He was just about to hang up when it was finally answered. Probably had gone to bed already, he mused.

"Hello?" A woman's tired voice. Niles got straight down to business.

"Listen carefully if you want the poodle back." He heard the now familiar gasp on the other end of the line when the person realised what was going on and the fact someone else was holding their beloved pet – for money. Her faint voice made him smile, the fact that he could wave his power over desperate people and they would follow his instructions perfectly amazed him; he loved the feeling it gave him. While he was only on the lower rungs of his chosen profession at the moment, he imagined what it would be like when the stakes were much higher, like children, women, things more precious to others than their stupid damn dogs.

He gave her the exact instructions, same as always, emphasising that if the police were told or involved in any way, the poodle would be gone – for good. She assured him that she would do exactly what was being asked of her, and the police would not be involved, she just wanted Bubbles back safe and sound. Satisfied, he hung up.

"Bubbles? What a rank name, silly cow," he mused out loud. Grabbing the house keys, he headed to the door, thinking. Tomorrow would be a decent payday, the gig a far more lucrative one than collecting scrap metal, but for now there was a pint waiting with his name on it and he set off to join the others.

Chapter Thirteen

IT WAS NEARLY 11pm when Ruth logged on to The Daisy Chain to moderate posts and comments, but she never minded the lateness. Being single and living alone meant every moment of the day or night was her own, to choose to do with what she pleased, and apart from work, it didn't matter when things got done. She'd devised the site some time ago and it was proving popular with the locals and growing in numbers daily. She was encouraged that she and the members were doing some good in the community. The first post caught her attention, Pam's dog had been found and Gemma was home safe and well from her adventure, whatever that had been.

"Thank god for that," she said.

From @Jaybaby – Good news, Gemma has been found #luckydoggy

@Belfort -Splendid news, any idea of the events, where she's been all this time?

@Jaybaby – nothing from me, saw Pam earlier tonight in the park with her. #Delighted

@Belfort – I guess it will remain a mystery, wonder where they go and why?

@Jaybaby – likewise, but at least she's home and well. Mystery solved. Time to go, ciao.

Ruth smiled at Gemma being home. Knowing exactly who @Belfort was, she couldn't help but grimace at his mock Italian sign off. Men found him funny, women found him repulsive and 'ciao' did not sound sexy coming from that man's mouth. Ruth scrolled down some more and was sad to see another dog was missing, this time a white poodle by the name of Bubbles. She read the post which stated she'd been lost from the park yesterday, hadn't come back when called and was a much loved family pet, the little ones missing her terribly. The picture that was posted showed the white poodle, tongue hanging out looking the epitome of a happy little dog.

"That's strange, another one missing. And from the park near Pam." She studied the time of the post, the description of what had happened and the picture of the missing poodle, trying to think of something useful that could help, but nothing came. Moderating the last of the day's posts and comments and finding nothing untoward, she closed the page down and sat thoughtful for a minute, chewing her bottom lip as she did so, something she'd done since she was a child, and something she found helped her think. Two dogs missing, same place, one returned. Maybe it was just a coincidence, but she bet herself the poodle would probably be back home either tomorrow or the day after, and when it did, it posed another question – what was happening?

Chapter Fourteen

LORNA STOOD LOOKING at the phone like it had been dropped in the hallway from outer space. In all her wildest dreams she'd never expected a ransom call for Bubbles, though in a perverse way she was pleased she had because that meant Bubbles was safe and well. One thing she did know from watching too many movies was that the culprits never harmed what they were holding hostage, the goods needed to be returned in one piece to get the money or it was no good, so in an odd way she was pleased to get the call. Bubbles would soon be home. When it had sunk in, she slowly made her way out to the kitchen at the back of the house, and sat in the window seat that overlooked the garden. Though she couldn't see anything out there in the dark, she could envision where everything in her garden was: the lovers' seat, the little stone fountain on the patio and the potting shed almost covered with Jasmine towards the back. She'd spent many hours tending to her garden, Bubbles enjoying the company and watching what Lorna was doing, and she missed her, like a good friend had left. Now she had another problem to deal with – getting the £4000 for tomorrow without her husband finding out, and then making the drop and getting her dog back – all on her own. She ran through the instructions in her head again to make sure she had everything they asked for, and while she thought she ought to tell the police, she wasn't going to jeopardise Bubbles.

"Let's get Bubbles back first and then I can decide what to do," she said out loud into the darkness. The kitchen light suddenly flicking on made her squint and jump at the same time. Her husband was standing in the doorway.

"Are you okay Lorna? Who was on the phone?"

She hated lying but right at that moment couldn't think about telling the truth.

"Wrong number, thought we were a taxi company and wouldn't take no for an answer," was the best she could come up with. She watched his face and he seemed to be satisfied with that, nodding in understanding. "You go up to bed, I'm not really that tired just yet for some reason, I think I'll make some Chamomile tea. You go back up, I'll be up soon," and she smiled as brightly as she could until he nodded again and turned to leave her sitting alone in the corner window seat. She turned her thoughts back to the problem at hand, how she'd raise the money, and the only solution she could come up with was she'd have to get the cash out on her credit cards. Then deal with explaining the expense later. When Bubbles was safely back, she was sure he'd understand.

The following day Lorna was at the cashpoint machine as soon as she'd dropped the little ones off at playgroup for the morning. She was grateful there was such a place because she'd already snapped at them both a couple of times. It hadn't gone unnoticed, it was totally out of character for her and she had ended up apologising to them both after tears had been spilled. Her mother was picking them up from playgroup and taking them back to her place for ice cream so Lorna could do what she needed to do without worrying about them at the same time. Her mother had been delighted, as most grandmothers are at the prospect of spoiling her grandchildren rotten, and was bringing them back after their afternoon nap. The machine spat out a bundle of £50 notes, all nice new crisp ones, and Lorna wondered at how little £2000 actually looked when it was in your hand. She slipped another credit card in and withdrew the same amount. Following the instructions, she put the money into an envelope then put the whole thing into her bag before heading home. She felt like a criminal, and a liar for fibbing to her husband last night. The kids still thought the dog was at the beauty parlour and her husband just thought the dog would wander back on her own. Thank goodness for a stressful job and a full mind that made him distracted sometimes. She made her way back to the house to busy herself until it was time for the drop at lunchtime.

Chapter Fifteen

Vic sat watching from her vantage point on the swings. She'd been there for over an hour, checking nobody else was setting up a lookout, nobody that resembled the police. It wouldn't be the first time that it had happened, and that had been a very sad day for the dog, the stupid owner having done exactly what they'd warned him not to, and his actions had had consequences. Lorna was obviously a bit brighter, or a bit more desperate. Vic watched as the blonde woman walked up the path towards the designated rubbish bin, looked around furtively, and dropped the envelope wrapped up in a Sainsbury's bag into the bin. The furtive glance made her smile. What was this, some bloody movie or something with the FBI watching? Nevertheless, she let Lorna walk on before she walked over to the bin and took the package to check it, and with £4000 tucked neatly in her jacket pocket, she texted Niles the drop had been done.

Almost immediately and from someplace up ahead in the bushes, a little white ball of woolly looking dog sprang out, yapping its little head off, and headed straight for Lorna. Hearing the familiar sound and spotting her little dog in the distance, Lorna instantly dropped to her knees to make a fuss of her Bubbles, her own screams of delight heard in all four corners of the park. Anyone watching would have seen an ordinary woman walking from the path on her own, and another woman making a huge fuss of a little white poodle, looking like she'd just found her long-lost friend. The little dog raced about, Lorna squealing with delight, though the tears rolling down her face may have looked out of place to anyone close enough to see them.

Vic left them to it, another job well done.

Chapter Sixteen

IT WAS three days later and Pam and Gemma were en route to the park for her afternoon runabout.

"Now then Gemma, we'll be there soon enough, you don't need to half drag me," she said to her little dog as they neared the front gate of the park, but Pam couldn't help smiling. It was delightful having Gemma back again, and June had volunteered to look after Gemma during the day while Pam worked so such an upsetting thing never happened again. Pam was extremely grateful to her friend and neighbour, and was now glad to be retiring a bit sooner because of what had happened. Never again would she let Gemma out of her sight, though she didn't think she was in any danger of being dognapped again by the same gang. Gemma turned to her looking for permission to run, and Pam slowly bent down to release her.

"Now Gemma, listen to me before you go." The little dog stood looking up at her, eyes bright, ears pricked and tongue hanging loose out of her mouth.

"You must stay close by, no disappearing into the bushes or I'll have to put you back on your leash, understand?" The little dog almost nodded her agreement and Pam gave her permission to run. Keeping her eye on her like a hawk, she slowly wandered to the nearby bench and sat at one end. As she sat, she realised it was the bench by the rubbish bin she'd done the drop in only a few days ago. The sting of tears filling her eyes was a painful memory of what she had nearly lost. Finding a handkerchief in her pocket, she dabbed them away before they could flood over, and blew her nose to shake herself back to the present. Gemma had kept to her word and was scampering about close by in the wide-open space, the deep green of the freshly mown grass a glorious contrast to her golden silky coat. She rested her head back and looked to the clear blue sky, then closed her eyes for a moment and said a little prayer of thanks. It was a woman's voice that brought her attention back to the park.

"Good morning, lovely isn't it?" Pam opened her eyes again and looked at the lady in front of her, recognising her as a regular dog walker though they had never spoken. Her little white poodle was by her feet. "May I sit here?" she enquired.

"Oh, good morning, please do, and yes it is lovely isn't it," Pam said, and watched the woman as she sat down, noting that her poodle was still on its leash. Gemma was still dashing about playing with a couple of fallen leaves and thoroughly enjoying herself nearby. Lorna spotted her and nodded her way.

"I'm not daring to let Bubbles off her leash at the moment, I lost her a few days ago, I've only just got her back so I'm a little untrusting of my surroundings at the moment. That's your Spaniel I presume?" she said, pointing with her head at Gemma. "She's a beautiful dog."

"Yes, she is. And it's odd that you should say you've only recently got yours back, because so have I. And I'm feeling a little nervous too, in fact today is the first time back in the park since she's been home." Pam realised the similarity straight away and turned to the woman and looked at her thoughtfully before she asked her a question. "Tell me if you don't mind, was your dog taken or lost?"

Lorna felt herself pale at the realisation that the woman she was sitting next to had possibly also been a victim —why else would she ask such a question?

"Taken. And I'm now guessing yours was too?"

"Yes. From my back garden, then a couple of days later they called and we did the exchange."

Lorna looked thoughtful for a moment before saying, "My goodness that must have been hell. Bubbles was only missing overnight and that was long enough. Come to think of it now, I remember seeing you the night you got her back because the first time I spotted you in the park you were alone, and then as I returned, you had her with you, making a real fuss of her. I was out looking for Bubbles." She went quiet for a moment then added, "My god! I wonder how many more there have been?"

Pam was thinking the same thing but how could they know for sure?

"They told me no police, but I'm wondering now if perhaps I should go back to them, I'm betting there's more than just us two victims. Trouble is, the dognappers know where I live."

"Then I should go and talk to them perhaps, let them know there is a gang out there taking advantage and making money off others' misery, it's not right, or nice."

Thinking for a moment, Pam wondered about The Daisy Chain. "There may be another way to find out who else has been affected before we go to the police, give us more ammunition as it were. They certainly weren't interested when Gemma first went missing, before I got the ransom call I mean. If we can tell them there are definitely more than two of us, they'll have to take notice and do something, won't they?"

"And what is that? What are you thinking?" Lorna asked.

"I'll post something on The Daisy Chain. I know the woman who runs the site, used to be a pupil of mine way back, she'll be able to help I'm sure."

"Great idea! Others might come out and share their experiences. That way, they can hide behind their user names for anonymity if they wish. And this gang, particularly if they're not local, won't know who they are, they probably don't even know about the site."

Pam turned to Lorna and smiled her agreement, and bent down to tickle Bubbles behind her ears.

"Hello Bubbles, I'm Pam, and that young lady over there is Gemma," she said pointing. "Pleased to meet you." Bubbles yapped just once in greeting back.

"And I'm Lorna, nice to meet you Pam," Lorna said, holding her hand out to shake. "Now let's get these mongrels caught before they strike again!"

"I agree. Let's see what surfaces after I post the question when I get back. There have got to be others, I'm sure of it."

They swapped phone numbers and agreed to meet in the park again at the same time tomorrow for an update. Hopefully they would have enough ammunition to go to the police with.

Chapter Seventeen

PAM WALKED BRISKLY BACK HOME like she was on a mission, which is exactly what she was on, much to Gemma's annoyance. Speeding back home was not what they usually did, and she much preferred the saunter where she could take her time sniffing posts and bushes before hanging out in the back garden for the rest of the day. But Pam had other thoughts today. It had been extremely upsetting when Gemma had gone and she didn't want others to suffer the same as she had. And now she had the chance to do something about the scumbags that were responsible for her and Lorna's distress. Though she didn't know for sure, she thought there would probably be others out there, unaware of this gang, and she was going to give them a chance to help catch the culprits.

It wasn't long before they were both back inside the small kitchen. She put the kettle on for tea and found her iPad, loading The Daisy Chain page as she waited for the kettle to boil. When the familiar click sounded, she poured hot water onto a chamomile bag and let it steep, taking it to the table out on the porch where she sat on her swing seat with Gemma beside her, iPad at the ready.

"Let's get this show on the road, eh Gemma? Those mongrels, pardon the pun, need to be caught, and soon. Let's see who else is out there."

She typed her post which read:

From @litlady – Gemma is home safe and well, thank you for all your help looking for her and your well wishes. But unfortunately, it doesn't end there. Gemma was stolen from me, and held for ransom. Yes, ransom! And Gemma and I are not the only ones to have been targeted. Only today I met a lady whose poodle had been stolen, also for ransom. We were both lucky enough to get our pets back but others might not be so lucky. Please, don't let your pets out of your sight! Don't give this gang, and I'm assuming there is more than one of them, the opportunity. And if you have had a similar experience, or know of anyone else that has, we need to know so the police can do something about it."

She tagged Ruth, the owner and moderator, in the conversation so she would definitely see it, and asked her a question at the same time.

"@McRuth, can people message you directly if they don't want to share publicly here? I'm assuming they can. Let's find these culprits and stop this nasty and very upsetting business."

She finished her piece and pressed 'post', then read through some of the other posts to see what else others were interested in. There were the usual harmless gossipy posts, largely about what the council had planned and people's viewpoints, someone had reported their underwear being stolen from their washing line again, and there was one report of a dog going missing only this morning. Pam's heart sank. The owners had posted a picture of him, with a heartfelt message pleading for information for his safe return. The little Jack Russell terrier looked a handsome boy, unimaginatively called 'Jack', but as Pam knew, his name was the least of his problems.

Looking down at Gemma who was laying by her side on the swing seat, she said "Ah Gemma, there is another one here, a little dog named Jack. We'll say a prayer for his safe return at bedtime. Let's hope they get him back safely soon." She took a final look at 'Jack', white with a distinctive tan patch, and closed her iPad down thoughtfully. She wished there was something she could do to help him, but what? There was no point contacting the owner directly just yet and telling them of her ordeal, it would only worry them further, and there was nothing to gain from it now, the dog had already been taken. The most she could do at this point was to warn others to keep alert, that is until anyone else came forward. She hoped they would.

Chapter Eighteen

"Not a bad week's work team, nearly £6000 here. Beats collecting shitty scrap metal and getting sod all for it, eh?" Niles was sitting counting the week's takings like the giant in *Jack and the Beanstalk*, a limp cigarette smouldering in the corner of his mouth, his thin wrinkled smoker's lips keeping it pressed into place. The air in the small lounge room was thick with his chain-smoking and the grey haze clung to everything and gave everyone a permanent stale cigarette smoke odour. Pete hated it when he smoked in here, why couldn't he piss off outside like everyone else did these days, but he knew not to say anything. Riling him up was not a good move so he kept his head down and concentrated on his game. He was playing chess online with someone in Aberdeen and he was winning.

"Nice one." Vic nearly always agreed with him and Pete wondered if she had a thing for him, though god knew why. Underneath her scruffy exterior she was a good-looking woman, although she needed to dress a bit more feminine, and the way she wore her greasy hair scraped tightly back didn't do her any favours. He knew without a doubt she could do a lot better than fancying Niles. And do a lot better with herself. Pete had tried to keep himself clear of the Niles' of this world but a couple of spells in juvie had put paid to that – the people he'd surrounded himself with involuntarily were all like Niles or younger versions of. Once you had a record not many employers wanted to touch you. Pete had found himself getting involved for the cash cut – he had to live on something. That was two years ago and they'd been going from town to town, only moving on when it got too hot to stay around. He knew time here was getting close to up, it wouldn't be long before someone suspected something and they'd be on the move yet again.

"Right, time for a pint, who's coming?" Pete watched Niles' cigarette bobbing up and down as he spoke.

"I'm in," said Vic, and of course she would be. "What about you Pete, fancy a lemonade?" Vic and Niles chuckled.

Pete lifted his head up from his screen, "I'll be there in ten, I've nearly got this guy, game's nearly over now, so I'll see you down there."

"Suit yourself, come on then Vic, let's get 'em in," and they left Pete to it. As they left the dingy house, Pete breathed a sigh of relief and was grateful for a bit of time on his own. He got up and opened the windows to let some fresh air in then sat back down to finish his game.

The old backstreet pub was nearly empty so Niles and Vic had no problem getting a seat. Vic went straight to the bar to order their drinks. The place smelt like a mixture of stale beer, stale bodies and stale urine from the gents' toilets. It was a dive, but it was local. With nobody about, Niles chatted openly about the last couple of weeks' progress and how well they were doing.

"I'm just not sure how long we should stay here. There's

some good rich targets in these parts, better than some of the other outer London towns we've worked that's for sure. May as well have more money for the same risk, eh Vic?"

"Agreed, that last one with the sodding yappy poodle was nice and easy, though that damn dog kept me awake half the night. Could have wrung its bloody neck." She took a long swig of her Pernod and blackcurrant and opened her packet of cheese and onion crisps, crunching loudly as she filled her mouth with several at once. Little flakes of fried potato fell from her lips down to her lap.

"Mucky bugger Vic, you're losing half of 'em." Niles took a sip of his pint and went on, "I think we've probably only got one more week or so round here, then we should move on again before the pigs find out. Someone is bound to think they're cleverer than us and try and involve them, and that always gets messy. Remember the last time someone did that? Served 'em right not to get their little precious back, dumb shits."

Vic remembered it well, she'd had to get rid of it. The main bar door opened and she watched a heavyset man with thick well-inked arms enter the pub and take a seat at the bar. Probably a local, she guessed, and being on his own guessed rightly that he'd chat to the barman then read his paper that was rolled up in his hand. Visitors like Niles and Vic were usually at a table.

Niles got her attention back. "Na, I reckon another week then we're done. Move on further into Kent maybe, some big money there, might even have pedigree dogs we can charge even more for, what do reckon?"

"Whatever you think's best, Niles, you're the brains of this operation," she said, with one eye back on the stranger at the bar.

"Yeah, reckon that's about it, get another few dogs from round here, then off to more lucrative climates." Vic thought

THE CONTROLLER

she saw the man turn slightly at Niles' voice, he wasn't exactly being quiet about it even now there was someone else in the pub.

The door opened again and Pete walked in and went straight to the bar, looking over his shoulder at Vic and Niles to check the levels of their drinks. No need for a top up yet, he thought, so he didn't bother even offering. He waited until the barman returned and ordered himself a lager, choosing to stand at the bar for a moment to take his first mouthful. As he did so, he looked to the right at the man sitting at the bar on his own, taking in his tattoos and rough exterior. Though his mother had always taught him not to judge a book by its cover, sometimes it was hard not to. He took another sip and tried not to be obvious in his appraisal as he stood there, in no hurry to join the others. He could hear Niles talking about moving towns if things got hot, and so it seemed could the man. Pete was no stranger to body language 'tells' and he could see the man was listening in to their conversation. As Niles laughed at some story of a ransom that had gone wrong, the big man pulled his phone out and quietly made a call. Pete stayed close by, his ears stretching to hear to what was being said but it was impossible without being found out. He let it drop but stayed where he was, interested suddenly in his bar mat and in what was going to happen next. The man certainly didn't look like the police, even an undercover one, he'd seen enough in his few years to know what one looked like, the tell-tale signs. The man put his phone down and carried on half reading his newspaper, with one ear very obviously turned to the table nearby and their continued conversation.

Chapter Nineteen

THE BULKY TATTOOED man finished his pint then ordered another, using the barman as a distraction to turn around properly and look at the two occupants at the small table nearby. Two young wannabes, he figured, were trying to look cool, one with a cigarette hanging from the corner of his mouth, despite the fact that smoking wasn't allowed inside pubs, but the barman hadn't said anything and probably wouldn't by the ambient smell of the place. He took in the young man's badly bleached hair, his scrawny build and jittery disposition and he wondered if someone so skinny and nervy had a drug problem – it was usually a sign with the folks he came across. In his line of work they were never the smartly dressed corporate types, but usually the bottom feeders of life, which suited him down to the ground. The more desperate they looked, the more desperate they usually were.

He moved his attention to the woman, and it was obvious from her gaze she was awestruck by him, probably in love if you could call it that, though god only knew why. Not looking much of an oil painting that one. He couldn't see why she was so besotted with him, what drew her in, but it did. Her eyes were stuck to him, her half smile as she listened to his stories, her chin resting in her open palm balancing on an elbow on the edge of the cheap wooden table told him she was raptured. Inwardly he scoffed and called her a silly cow, but she probably didn't know much else, hadn't had much more experience in her life. Still, the two of them could prove to be useful, and from what he'd just heard, they already had a bit of experience. Now he just had to wait for the right moment to approach and put his proposal to them.

Niles and Vic had seen Pete walk in and order himself a lager but hadn't bothered to call him over. Vic for one wasn't about to, preferring instead to have Niles' attention all to herself. The Pernod and black had already started to have its effect on relaxing her, her tongue feeling a little numb from the aniseed spirit.

"Pete's just walked in and got himself a drink, cheeky sod, never asked if we wanted another round, tight arse." Niles took another drag on his cigarette, the thin grey mist hovering around his head like a foggy halo.

"Ah, leave him be, he's harmless enough, and until we need another target, we don't need him for much, and most of the time he's playing games on his sodding computer. He's a right geeky techie nerd. Where did you find him anyway?" Vic had often wondered how they'd all got to work together but until now had never asked, and put it down to the Pernod giving her balls.

"Came across him when he came out of juvie the second time I think. A bit of a set up like this," he said, waving his pint arm around the pub in a small semi circle. "I was having a pint someplace and he came in, and we got talking. He was looking for a job, and decided to drown his sorrows in a lemonade, that's why I tease him. No one ever wants to give an ex con, even a young 'un out of juvie, the time of day never mind pay 'em to do a job."

"So you approached him and took him under your wing then? What were you doing for money back then?"

"Ah you know, anything really. A bit of thieving to order, small stuff like flat-screen TV's, but it got a bit too intermittent and I needed a more reliable income stream so I came up with this. Since you and me met, it's been much easier to pull off, you being female and all, less suspect like. And we needed a lookout, that third person. Just means we can do more even though it's another person to split it with." She watched as he took another long drag on his cigarette, despite the disapproving looks from the barman, the smoke drifting straight up from the roll-up between his fingers. Vic put her glass to her lips and dropped her head back, draining the glass loudly like she was gurgling the remains of a milkshake through a straw.

"Steady on Vic, it's not lemonade you know, you're supposed to sip it," he said, smiling through his words. "You want another?"

"Yes, why not. It's warmed my insides nicely, might need a lie down when we get back," and she smiled sweetly at him, trying to catch his eyes, though by the neutral look on his face as he stood, he hadn't picked up on her flirt to join her. Either that or he wasn't interested. The man at the bar on the other hand understood her body language and innuendo perfectly. As Niles reached the bar to order, the man took the opportunity and opened the conversation.

"She's certainly into you, my man, know what I mean? Got it bad I'd say."

"Eh? What do 'ya mean, and what's it to you anyhow?" Niles always took the defensive line first, something he'd picked up inside the very first time he'd ended up there. He'd also learned to mind his own business, unlike this wise guy.

"Just an observation, mate, that's all. And not a bad looker either, though that's not why I'm talking to you."

"Oh yeah? And why's that then?" Still overly cocky, which amused the man, and it showed.

"Look, knock the hard man shit off, will you, I might be able to put a bit of business your way and you me, like. Help each other out." Niles dropped the attitude a little but stayed on his guard.

"You a pig?"

The man chucked. "Do I look like a sodding pig? No, thought not. But I have been eavesdropping for the past half-hour about your dog scam. You know, you should talk quieter, someone might overhear you and drop you in it."

"Is that a threat then, is it?" The attitude was back.

"No, but an observation. Look, I have an idea. And it means you can double dip, so a win win for us both."

"I'm listening."

"You still do your ransom bit, get your dough, and instead of giving the dogs back, you on sell the dogs on to me."

Niles thought for a moment before he responded. If he understood this man correctly, they still kidnapped the dog, but when they'd paid up, they never got them back because he on sold them to this guy? Sounded alright to him. And easy.

"How much each you talking?"

"Well, let's say £100 each. That's an extra £100 profit for the same work, less work in fact. No need to risk dropping the dog back."

"£100 is peanuts actually." Niles was shaking his head in agitation. Who was this guy wasting his time?

"Yes but it's a regular £100. I need a regular supply see, they go all over the UK, big business for what I need them for. You interested or not? Because if you're not, I'll look elsewhere."

Niles could never turn a deal down and another £100 per

dog for doing not much else, and regular too, would soon add up nicely. He thought for a moment longer.

"Okay, you're on. What do you need and when do you need it?" Niles was beginning to get excited as the sums added up in his head. The big man gave him a brief smile, asked for his telephone number and said someone would be in touch tomorrow with the first order, then turned back to his pint, leaving Niles in his excited state still standing next to him but ignored. Niles took the hint, ordered another pint for him and a Pernod and black for Vic, and completely ignored Pete at the other end of the bar – two could play at that game. He felt pleased with himself, he now had a lucrative sideline to their operation and he needed to think through some of the logistics, so he gathered both their drinks and went to tell Vic about his conversation and their new plan.

From where Pete was standing he'd heard every damn word and his blood was boiling in his veins. One thing about spending time on the wrong side of the law meant that he'd learned a few things inside juvie. If his suspicions were right, he knew exactly where this fresh supply of dogs was going. And that repulsed him.

Chapter Twenty

"Oh Gemma, look," Pam said, pointing to her iPad screen as if the dog could read, understand and comment. "There are a couple of comments from other people that have had their pets stolen and held to ransom. If those are the ones that have come forward, I bet there are still others." Pam scrolled down the page and read further: two missing dogs but both had been returned after a phone call, the dogs being of sentimental value and much-loved members of the family rather than pedigrees. Maybe dognapping pedigree pups and dogs wasn't as lucrative, Pam wondered, that or they were much harder to steal – pedigree breeders tended to have better security than the average dog owner. Still, whatever the reason, it made Pam feel sick to her stomach that this was happening in their neighbourhood. She composed a private message to Ruth:

"Ruth, let's alert the police now we have more victims, there's obviously a gang doing the rounds and they need to be stopped. When can you go? I'll come with you and I'll see if Lorna can come too, they have to listen now."

She signed off with her name and hit send and waited for a response. While it was quite late in the evening, Pam knew that Ruth was a bit of a night owl, and suspected she might still be up. She was right. Ruth had seen her message and replied almost instantly:

"Pam, Agree. We'll go at lunchtime tomorrow if you can make that, see if Lorna can. See you outside the station at 12.30? Ruth"

Pam texted Lorna the plan. Since she wasn't sure if the rest of the family had been told about the demand and dognapping, she thought a quick text at this hour would be safest, a phone call a little harder to explain. Lorna responded almost instantly with a "yes, see you there," and the first part of getting the horrible experience sorted was under way.

At 12.30pm the following day Pam, Lorna and Ruth met up and went inside the police station and spoke to the desk sergeant. Pam remembered the man from when she had tried to report Gemma stolen. She hoped that this time he would be a bit more helpful and take them more seriously. He smiled as she approached the desk.

"Yes, I remember you from a few days ago, good to see you got your dog back. That her tied up outside the door?" he asked, pointing with his disposable pen.

"Yes, it is, and that's why we are here," said Pam. It was decided before they all went in that Pam would do the talking first as she was a victim and had already spoken to the police before. "She was in fact stolen, and so have at least five other dogs that we now know of." That got his attention.

"Tell me what you know, Mrs...?"

"It's Pam Davies, Sunnymead Road. Just call me Pam."

"Well Pam, tell me more." His pen was poised.

"As you know, my Gemma was missing, and two days after she first went, I got a call, a ransom call in fact, and they wanted £500 dropped in a bin in the park then I'd get Gemma back. And before you ask why I didn't come to you, he told me, that is, the man that called, if I went to the police, if there was any sign of them present, I'd never see her again. So I didn't tell you." The sergeant scowled a little, taking notes for his report.

"Go on, please."

"Well, I did as requested, dropped the money, then out of nowhere came Gemma. I never saw anybody and there was no more contact with them. I was just so happy to get her back unscathed. But it seems I'm not the only victim."

Lorna stepped forward to add to the story, the sergeant now taking a keener interest at the word ransom. "Bubbles was taken too, and I also got a call, that same night, and they wanted £4000."

The desk sergeant's eyebrows cocked in disbelief. £4000 was a hell of a lot more than £500, but he didn't say as much. He carried on with his note-taking and Lorna carried on talking.

"I too dropped money into a bin in the park and from nowhere Bubbles came out of the bushes. Just like Pam, I simply wanted my girl home safe and well. I haven't even told my family yet and I too was threatened not to contact the police. And there's more people that have had the same experience."

It was Ruth's turn to contribute. "Afternoon, officer. I'm Ruth McGregor and I don't have a dog, but I do run the local online site The Daisy Chain. You may or may not be aware of it?"

"Can't say as I am aware, sorry. What is it exactly and how does it fit here?"

"It's something I set up a while back, sort of a community page where locals post comments: suspicious activities, general neighbourly chatter, anything that could be useful to others, that sort of thing."

He nodded to go on.

"Well, I asked the online group, there are a couple of thousand of us now, if anyone had lost their dog recently and then had it returned, without going into too much detail publicly. And here's the thing, two more people have come forward to say they had fallen foul of these people, and there is a little Jack Russell missing as we speak, making it five so far. I suspect there will be more, not everyone will have seen the post to respond, or don't want to get involved."

Ruth relaxed a little after telling him what she knew. All three of them waited in silence, wondering what he would say. Would the police now take this seriously?

"Right then, looks like there's something needs investigating properly now."

The women breathed a collective sigh of relief. "I'm going to just get all your contact details, fill in a bit more information, then pass it on to one of my colleagues to look into. Shall I put yourself as the main contact point? Since you are involved but not a victim, it might just be easiest." He was looking directly at Ruth as he spoke and she nodded her approval.

"Yes, that's fine with me. In the meantime, I'll watch for more people coming forward, let's hope there aren't too many," and everyone agreed.

The sergeant finalised the last of the details he needed and told Ruth an officer would be in touch later that day and they'd set the ball rolling. He watched as the three women left the front reception area, sucking on the end of his cheap pen in thought. He didn't like the sound of this one little bit, these things usually escalated into something worse and they needed to catch this gang before it did so or before they moved on again. He picked up the report and headed out back to the main squad room.

"You got a minute?" he asked the female detective passing by.

"Sure, what you got?"

"Four cases of dognapping for ransom, and another suspected, all local people. In my experience it can get ugly if not taken care of. You able to look into it?"

Amanda took the report and quickly scanned through it. She'd seen this sort of thing before and also knew it rarely ended well. She ran her fingers through her short cropped hair. Bits stood out at odd angles.

"Thanks Doug, I'm on to it. I'll go round later today and see what else I can dig up. Sounds like this website could be helpful too. Who's the main contact?" she asked, scanning the page again.

"It's Ruth McGregor, do you know her?"

"Not yet I don't."

Chapter Twenty-One

AMANDA WALKED up the front path of the Richmond road address and rapped on the brass doorknocker, hearing the heavy sound echo back though the quiet street. Doorbells were probably a little more noise friendly – this rapper informed the whole street that someone was knocking on the McGregor door. She could hear footsteps coming from inside, on what sounded like a wooden floor, and the Detective was glad she didn't have to rap the brass knob again. As the door opened, Amanda was ready with her credentials in her hand.

"Afternoon. Ruth McGregor? I'm DS Amanda Lacey."

"Oh, yes, please, come on inside." Ruth stood to one side of the door to allow the detective entrance, and held her arm out to show the way inside and down the hallway. "Thanks for coming round. Can I get you a drink, tea, lemonade perhaps?"

"Lemonade would be great, thanks. I'm a bit 'tea'd' out at this time of day and it's actually quite warm outside." They chatted easily as they walked through the house.

Ruth pointed to the back of the house and the open back door. "Please, take a seat on the patio and I'll bring it out for you. It's such a lovely afternoon, a shame not to take advantage of it." Amanda made herself comfortable on one of the wicker chairs under the large umbrella and looked out onto the garden. She called over her shoulder back to Ruth in the kitchen.

"Great place you've got here and such a fabulous garden."

"Thanks. I'd like to say it's all my own work but it isn't. I just potter around, with the few herbs and tomatoes being my contribution. Not enough time I'm afraid," she said, as she put two glasses of lemonade down on the table. "Though I love fresh herbs in my cooking and tomatoes are great all year round, so I bottle pasta sauce with the excess for winter. Do you garden?"

"No, my place is very low maintenance, comes with the territory of being a detective. Never enough hours in the day." Amanda took a long sip of her lemonade. She groaned with satisfaction. "This is outstanding! From your lemon tree?" she said enquiringly, noting the abundance of lemons hanging from a small tree sheltered at the edge of the patio.

"Thanks, and yes they are, glad you like it." Ruth couldn't help feeling something had clicked into place as this woman chatted to her so easily, but flicked the thought from her mind like you would a piece of lint from your trousers. Amanda must have had a similar thought because suddenly she was all business. Clearing her throat, she started.

"So tell me about The Daisy Chain, and how it fits in with Pam and Lorna's experience."

"It was started a few months back, I'm in IT, I work for myself, and it seemed a useful thing to do, bring a community together for help and advice, and it's sort of blossomed into quite a thriving place. I moderate it, with the help of another moderator, Benjamin, so we can keep it family friendly and on track. We don't tolerate unsubstantiated gossip, bad language or racism. It's there as a place to meet and contribute."

Amanda nodded and Ruth went on, "When Pam's dog Gemma went missing, she asked for help looking for her and for people to keep an eye out, that sort of thing."

"And now you know through this community that others have had similar experiences too?"

"Yes, we asked if anyone else had recently lost their dog and then got it back under unusual circumstances, meaning that those that had fallen prey to this gang would know what we meant but others wouldn't and be worried. Seemed like the right way to approach it. And two came forward. The little Jack Russell to my knowledge is still missing." Ruth watched Amanda scribbling notes in her pocket notebook.

"Well, from what we know so far, this only started recently so we'll suppose this gang has only just moved into the area. How long they stay is anyone's guess, though I know of these gangs from experience. Some of them are pretty nasty. Pet ransoms have a habit of turning into something much bigger as the gang gets more confident and it's not unknown for dogs to be stolen, ransom demands made but then the animal finds itself in a far worse situation, never going back home despite payment being made. It's quite horrific. Can you get the details of the two that came forward online? I'll need to get statements from them too."

"Absolutely, now they have their pets back I'm sure they'll help but you can understand why none of these people came forward as it was happening. Not nice to have your family pet go missing. I'll message them both as soon as you leave. What's the best way to contact you?"

Amanda handed Ruth her card. "Mobile is best, or email if it's more convenient for you, it's all on there. I'm going to join the group and watch for myself and see what comes up, just so you're aware, but let's keep in touch with developments and if you think of anything else, just let me know. I'll also be going back to Pam and Lorna, see if they can remember anything else, even smallest of details can help." She smiled brightly at Ruth as she stood to leave and Ruth returned the gesture. "And thanks for the delicious lemonade. I'll be in touch," and she slowly walked back down the hallway towards the front door, her own footsteps now audible on the polished floor.

"I'll get the door for you," said Ruth and squeezed past her to do so. "Where are my manners?" With the front door wide open, Amanda left the house and followed the front path back down to the curb and her waiting car. Ruth stood in the doorway and watched as Amanda drove off, giving a little wave through the passenger side window as she did so. Ruth was glad of her visit, that something would now be done to find the culprits and stop any more heartache, but as she closed the front door, she also realised she was just as glad to have met Amanda.

Chapter Twenty-Two

RUTH AWOKE the following morning with the sun streaming through her bedroom window. It was something she always loved to see, and it made getting up a whole lot easier and much more pleasant. As she came to, and stretched like a cat on a lazy Saturday morning, she wondered if the little Jack Russell was back at home with its owners yet. That would be a nice start to the weekend for them all. She let her mind wander to what the detective, Amanda, had said about things progressing in the wrong direction for these gangs. She knew she had to do something more to help, but what exactly? She couldn't attach herself to the police force just because it suited her to do so, and she was no private detective on her own, but could she somehow use her IT skills to do good? Ideas entered her mind slowly and as each one was disregarded, she was left with just one. Could she pose for a dognapping victim herself with the aid of the police, and a GPS-chipped dog? Would that work? As she thought more about it, she realised neither she nor the police knew anything about where this gang hung out or what they were looking for so that probably wouldn't work, and it was too damn risky. Then it hit her. She leapt out of bed, headed downstairs to the kitchen, grabbed her iPad, a pen and paper and put a capsule in the coffee machine. With the smell of fresh coffee in the background, she made a list of everything she knew about the four victims so far, where the dogs were taken from and what each dog's breed was. Anything she could think of went down on the paper. Then she looked at what she had. While there was no common denominator in the breed, they were all small dogs. The majority were taken from the park without their owners seeing anything, and they all got a phone call within 48 hours, though Lorna's was within 24. Ransom demands were between £500 and £4000, that being the most and that being Lorna's. So what was so different there then, why the larger amount? She looked at the addresses of the other victims and Lorna's stood out for one reason – The Heath. It was an expensive area. If the gang knew this, they must have known where she lived. Pam's Gemma was taken from her home, a small house on a regular street, and as she was the oldest victim, that must have been the reason for the smallest ransom. The answer was obvious. The gang knew things about their targets *beforehand*; it wasn't just a random snatch. She opened The Daisy Chain on her iPad and checked for replies to her post on missing dogs. Three more people had come forward and so she messaged them back to get the details to add to her list. The puzzle was coming together but within a few minutes there was a private message from someone else.

"Holy shit," she said out loud, and her heart sank a little as she read the message. A ransom drop had been made last night but the little dog had not been given back, even though the owners had done everything the caller had asked. They feared they might now never see their dog Jack again. This changed everything.

Chapter Twenty-Three

LIONEL CLICKED THE LITTLE RED 'x' and closed the web page down. He sat thoughtfully at the kitchen table, chewing the little piece of skin that always seemed to stick out by the nail on his middle finger of his left hand, then glanced at the surrounding area of the offending piece of skin. It was the colour of the inside of a ruby grapefruit. He picked his mug up and swigged back the remains of his second coffee of the day and wondered about what he'd just read. He was putting two and two together. He'd heard of gangs like this before but had never had any dealings with them himself. It wasn't his scene, he'd never agreed with them.

Thinking back to the posts he'd just read, he knew all too well that a ransom gang was in town and it wouldn't be long before either a copycat group set up and took things to the next level, or they were approached by someone to do the job themselves – for an extra fee. And gangs liked extra fees. And he thought he knew just who the person doing the approaching might be. MacAlister – his boss.

Lionel knew his boss wasn't the most scrupulous of businessmen but he had never actually *seen* him do anything wrong, but then he wouldn't be likely to. MacAlister was smart, and rough, the type of guy you didn't ever question. As long as Lionel did his job and kept his nose out, they both got along just fine. So that's what he did, but that didn't stop his mind whirring round. He knew that MacAlister had been involved in illegal gambling before, it was good money, but he'd managed to keep himself out of bother. Lionel had long since suspected MacAlister had a friend on the inside that owed him, and that someone kept a blind eye turned as repayment for his debt. Or for a bung. A policeman's wage was okay but nothing special and there was always someone in need of the extra cash, you just had to find out who it was. And why. Then you had them.

Lionel closed the computer down, grabbed his car keys and left the house. He headed for the bookies in the village where he worked, the dognapping business very much on his mind. He'd have a look and do some research when it got quieter later in the morning. For some reason, a word had jumped into his head, something floating in his sub conscious – Chatham. Maybe a punter had mentioned something to do with dogs there recently? He couldn't be sure but he'd double-check the significance of it when he got a minute. It was just a town in Kent, wasn't it? No harm in looking. But for now, he had a bookies to run, and as he pulled into the small car park at the back of the shop, there was already a car parked there. He instantly recognised the striking high-end Range Rover, wrapped in a menacing-looking matt black paint job and complete with tinted windows – it belonged to Mac MacAlister. If a vehicle could look like its owner, this one certainly did.

"What the hell does he want?" Only one way to find out.

Chapter Twenty-Four

"MORNING MAC," Lionel said as he entered the office through the old back door. He was always civil even if he didn't really like or trust the man – he wanted to stay in the job, so he sucked it up.

"Morning Lionel. Just dropped by to grab some cash, I'd hoped you hadn't banked it yet."

"No, you've beat me to it." Lionel watched as MacAlister counted out a bunch of £20 notes into several piles on the cheap old Formica table, a hundred in each he guessed, and there were already 10 piles lined up in front of him.

"Looks like someone's about to spend up large today, going some place nice with the missus?"

MacAlister carried on counting and Lionel wished he hadn't said anything. The only sound was the slight scrapping of the crinkled paper on paper. It seemed an age before he said anything. In a low concentrated voice he said, "Got a little something going on tonight out at Chatham, need to get the dough there before then, don't need to be seen with it."

There was that word again, the one that had popped into his head earlier – Chatham. Lionel knew it would be something shady, it always was, and he kept his own head down and his own nose clean and well out of Mac's business. He could do what he wanted; Lionel was only interested in his wage at the end of the week and a curry every now and then.

"Well, good luck with it then, I'll put a note in the banking so you know when it gets tallied up later. In case you forget like." MacAlister raised his head from gathering the cash up and glared at Lionel, who withered visibly under his gaze.

"Don't bother," was all he said before he pocketed the cash and headed for the back door. So Lionel didn't. But that didn't stop him not liking it.

Chapter Twenty-Five

WITH HIS DRONE all set Jim headed out, with Duke, his Alsatian, close by his side.

"Where do you fancy this morning, the fields or the woods?" Jim glanced down at his best friend as he chatted and Duke didn't disappoint with the answer. A single bark, it could have been either destination or something unrelated, so Jim made his own mind up, smiling at the stupidity of asking his dog and guessing the answer. But he knew he wasn't the only one who did it. All pet-lovers do it, whether the owner is talking to a terrapin or a tarantula.

He clipped the dog's leash on and they set off down the quiet country road, headed for the woods, which meant crossing several fields he had no right to be in. Although there were plenty of notices posted about stating 'Private Property' on fences and gate posts, he chose to ignore them. He wasn't doing any harm, just walking his dog.

They'd been walking for about 10 minutes when Jim decided to stop and set his drone up for flight. He loved technology, and his latest drone fascinated him with its capabilities. It could even live stream to Facebook if he wanted it to, though because he didn't exactly keep to aviation rules, he didn't think he'd ever do it. Anyway, it recorded its view to a card internally if you activated it, so there could be a record should he need it. No point advertising to the world he was breaking rules, and being in places he really shouldn't be.

The familiar whir as the four propellers started was like music to his ears. He made his control selections before allowing the clever eye-in-the-sky to fly off. He could see from the screen in his hands exactly what the drone could see, and it fascinated him how the same place that he was standing could look so different from just a few feet up. He took it higher and at 50 feet he could see himself in the field at the control pad, Duke by his side.

"Come on Duke, let's see what we can see today." They both set off towards the woods in the near distance, the drone's sensors more than capable of steering itself clear of any obstacles such as power poles and trees. From his screen, he could see way ahead of himself. The drone was now totally out of his sight, probably about half a mile away, and looking so small in the sky, most people would never even know it was there.

The long grass up past his knees was making it quite slow going, though Duke was happy nipping backwards and forwards to his master as they both ventured towards the thick woodland. Watching the view on his screen, he was in awe of the view, the thick canopy of the woods above his head but below the clever eye, the mass of thick dark green blowing gently in the wind. Birds were leaving high-up branches in a hurry as the whirring machine passed nearby, and then he spotted a clearing. He stopped still for a moment while he navigated the drone back a little and had a look around the small open space that was somewhere up ahead of him. He could see the woodland floor, a few half-rotten tree stumps where trees were had been removed or had fallen over, and what looked like a small decrepit wooden shed. Still without moving, he brought the camera in closer and circled inside the clearing, There wasn't too much else to see but he made a note of the coordinates anyway. Some people collected train numbers, some people collected GPS coordinates of things that piqued their interest. Jim was the latter and had never understood the former. While he considered himself a nerd, he was a techie nerd not an anorak train-spotter nerd.

He could hear Duke barking somewhere further on in the trees and called him back.

"Duke!" he shouted. The last thing he wanted while he was trespassing was for his dog to give him away, so he tried calling him again with a little more urgency in his voice. But Duke was ignoring him.

"Damn it Duke! Keep it down would you," he shouted, and started off in the direction the barking was coming from, gathering speed as the long grass and undergrowth allowed.

"Duke! Here boy, come!" Still the dog ignored his command but Jim was getting closer, the dog's bark was getting louder.

"Duke! Come here. Duke!" He pushed his way through the low branches and prickly bushes, having left the drone to circle above nearby while he made his way to get his dog. He could just see him in the distance.

"Duke! Shush will you and come here! Duke!" The dog was not happy at something, and Jim he approached him, he could see the hairs standing up on the back of his neck, a low growl interspersing his barks, his tail showing he was upset. Jim made his way over, talking calmly now to his dog, aware something was worryingly wrong – he never acted like this usually. Duke turned and saw him but carried on barking, trying to tell Jim what was bothering him. As Jim scanned the nearby surroundings, he finally saw what Duke was so upset by. Realisation dawned at what he was looking at, and as Duke finally quieted down in his presence, Jim couldn't stop himself. He bent over and heaved his breakfast up in three violent spasms.

"The sick bastards."

When he finally recovered, he took note of the GPS coordinates of his location and got the hell out of there, taking Duke with him as quickly as he could.

Chapter Twenty-Six

"Look Pete, I know what I was looking at, I just don't know what I can do about it. Not only do I have a police record, I was trespassing and using a drone illegally, but I can't sit back and do nothing. They're real sick bastards but I don't know how I can fix this without landing myself in it."

Pete thought for a moment before replying to his friend's message.

"I'm guessing an anonymous tip-off wouldn't work?"

"No, I think we need to get more evidence first. What I saw could have come from anywhere, though I assume it was local. I'm going to ask around a little, see if I can find out more, then drop them in it maybe."

"Look Jim, I wouldn't do that, that sounds dicey, too risky. Did you record it while you were there?"

"I got the coordinates so I know exactly where it is but I didn't record it, no. But I see what you're getting at."

Pete confirmed the idea. "Send the drone back in to record it, but keep well back, and then send me the file. I'll find someone this end who can help, I'll keep it anonymous.

We've both got records to think about but we can't leave this."

Pete could almost feel Jim relax a little at his end. Even in juvie, Jim had always been the anxious one, not the villain he tried to portray, a bit like Pete in that respect. Somewhere, life had knocked the points handle of his tracks and his engine and carriages had gone hurtling in the wrong direction, not unlike Pete's, destination 'trouble.' They'd kept in touch when they'd come out of juvie, and while they didn't see each other in person much, they talked in various chat rooms and via Messenger. They both found socialising way much easier that way.

"Thanks Pete, I knew you'd figure it out, always was the brighter one. I'll get it done tomorrow and let you have it. I'll send you the link, stick the file in the cloud."

"Great, now don't say a word, let the drone do the work tomorrow, and for god's sake, stay out of sight."

"Got that."

They signed off and Pete sat looking at his screen. His chess game had turned to shit so he made his last move that pretty much finished the game anyway, the other guy the winner. His mind hadn't been on it when Jim told him what he'd seen and he was starting to put two and two together and come up with four. He knew that Niles was up to something, ever since he'd overheard the conversation in the pub with the tattooed man, though he'd never let on he had heard. Add that to the fact that that last ransom drop hadn't gone as normal either. They'd got the money okay but Vic hadn't handed the dog back, saying she thought someone was loitering in the park, maybe a plain-clothed policeman, and she hadn't wanted to risk it.

"Better to be safe than sorry," she'd explained to him, so the dog was still in the basement. When he'd asked Niles how they were going to get it back to the owner, he'd simply laughed in his face, cigarette smoke swirling from the ever-present paper roll in the corner of his mouth. For some reason, Vic and Niles had chosen not to include him in their plan. That meant they didn't trust him but he could hardly call them out on it otherwise they'd know he knew. He didn't like the feel of how things were heading and now he suspected they were in something deeper with this other man. He thought he knew the answer, but needed confirmation, and a plan. Pete switched off his computer and sat back in his cheap mock leather chair to think – he needed to put this right. And soon.

Chapter Twenty-Seven

"SHUT THE HELL UP, WOULD YOU!" The man turned round and shouted behind the driver's seat in the van. "I can't do with that noise all the damn way!"

In the back of his small van were four small rusty metal cages, each holding a dog, each one barking its lungs out. The sound was deafening in the small space of the old van and the driver couldn't normally care less, but today he had a banging headache and the dogs were only adding to his pain.

He turned off the narrow road, bumping along an unsealed single track lane that led to his final destination, the old van bouncing from side to side as it went. No one would ever stumble across the place where he was headed, which was one of the reasons it had been picked, yet if you knew where to look, it wasn't that hard to find. And for what they used the property for, they needed certain people to be able find it or else it didn't make any money. But not the cops.

A couple of miles further on, at the end of the dirt track, the driver came to a standstill just outside the largest of a group of buildings. He headed over to the front entrance, gravel crunching underfoot, dust drifting upwards. He wiped the sweat from his brow on the back of his shirt sleeve and spat into the dirt. The wooden building was vast, like a huge barn, the tin roof looking in need of repair, the two massive old double doors at the front fully open to let the light in. No one was around so he shouted out.

"You there Tony?" He stepped inside the barn and tried again. "Yo!"

Nobody shouted back so he ventured a little further in, past the necessary equipment, the pens and the cages, some occupied, others empty. A large heavyset man made his way toward him, with hardly any blank space left on the vast amount of tattooed bare chest. The van driver held his hand out in greeting.

"Tony, good to see you," he said. The big man shook. "I've got a delivery for you, where do you want 'em?"

"Stick 'em at the back, some empties there. Won't be needing them just yet. How many?"

"Got four," he said, smiling a blackened tooth smile. "That little white sod won't last long," he said spitefully, but Tony ignored his comment, he really didn't care as long as it served its purpose when the time came.

"Right, I'll square up later. You comin' tonight?"

"Hell yeah, hoping for a big night. Got a bit to spend for a change. Found the bitch's housekeeping money too." He smiled at the big guy, his two blackened front teeth and badly bleached short hair making him look a lot like a yellow ferret. "And I've got money here from MacAlister, he wants £500 on Jaxton and another on that Japanese dog, can't think of it's damn name, you know the one I mean. He'll be up later but wanted me to put the two bets on now, so he's not seen like." He handed over the cash to Tony, who slipped it into his trouser pocket.

"Right then," Tony said, slapping the young driver on the back, "Now drive in and unload 'em and I'll see you later on then. I got work to do before then so I need you to piss off, alright?" Tony half smiled to the driver, a simple disposable who'd worked with him for a couple of years but really was as thick as pig shit. He was good enough for what he needed him to do though, cheap labour. As long as he kept his gob shut. Tony watched him unload and drive back out of the barn, a quick nod of his head through the driver's side window as he left.

"Silly prick," Tony said out loud to the retreating van. He went back to the little room he'd had built within the barn, what he called his office, and back to his flat-screen TV and soccer match. Spurs were playing West Ham, always a tense game, and this one was no different. He wished he were there in the crowd. There was always a scuffle or two and he enjoyed a brawl occasionally, good for relieving stress. And for keeping up appearances, a man like him had a brand to maintain. He settled back in his old leather chair, crossed his ankles up on the desk in front of him and rested his hands behind his head. And there he stayed for the remainder of the match.

Chapter Twenty-Eight

WHILE HE DIDN'T WANT to go back into the woods, Jim knew he had to get some proof. This time he was armed with a plan, because he didn't want to be caught hanging around where he shouldn't be and land himself in more trouble than just trespassing. Getting involved accidentally with the men that ran these types of things was not something he relished the thought of, he knew from stories from other inmates how nasty those bastards could be.

Taking Duke for both protection and an excuse for looking like an innocent dog walker, he confirmed the co-ordinates for the drone, clicked the record option and sent it on its way, following on foot via the screen in his hands. If he stayed a good way off, he shouldn't be spotted. That was his simple plan. He just hoped to hell it went smoothly.

Ten minutes into the woods, he had found what he had seen yesterday, and while it turned his stomach again to look, he had to get the footage of it, so he brought the drone down for close-up shots taken from the safety of the edge of the woods.

"Got it," he said to Duke, who was still on his leash by Jim's feet, not daring to let him off while he did what he needed to do. But last night lying in his bed, thinking about what he had to do today, he'd had another thought. What he had found meant that the source had to be some place nearby, it made sense. He looked at Duke for confirmation.

"Let's just take a quick look around from here with the drone. We're safe as long as we keep a lookout, I can easily send the drone in further for a quick scout round. What do you say?" Duke just looked up at Jim and panted.

"You're not a lot of use, boy, are you," he said gently, scratching his dog behind his ear. "Good job I'm on the case to make the decisions." He steered the drone out of the trees and further on, scouting round for anything that might catch his interest, though he wasn't sure what that would look like. Then he saw it up ahead.

"Bingo Duke, I think we may have something." He brought the drone down a little lower as it approached what had taken his interest and he could see the building in detail. It was wooden with what looked like a rather rough tin roof and had two massive front doors that stood wide open. The pictures being fed to his small screen made his heart race and he was glad he was recording it all. As the drone flew down lower and approached the two big open doors, he could see a lot more of the operation, but he was conscious of the drone's noise raising awareness of its intrusion and he was ready at a moment's notice to swing it out of there, at record speed if he had to. He felt comfortable that no one would know it was he at the controls. Jim let out the breath he'd been holding involuntary and tried to relax a little as he filmed. The drone slowly scouted around the outside of the building one more time to double-check if anyone was around before he sent it inside. From where he was standing hidden in the trees he couldn't hear a thing apart from the sound of his heart beating hard and fast in his chest. He let the drone go inside, and quickly did a 360-degree circle, then he got it the hell out of there. He didn't want to hang around any longer than he had to and could look at the footage later – now was not the best time. As far as he was aware, nobody had been alerted to the drone's presence and he brought the machine back to where he was standing, safe in the knowledge he had some decent evidence – all recorded. He slipped the drone back into his backpack and left the woods with Duke at his side, still looking like any other random dog walker.

When they got back home Jim took a proper look at what he'd filmed and his suspicions were confirmed. From the bird's-eye view from the camera, he'd taken all he needed as evidence. Now he had to do the right thing with it. He loaded the file into a folder in the cloud and messaged Pete the link to access it.

"Got what we needed, and more. Take a look and do your best with it. From what I've seen now I've looked properly, it's set up for fairly soon. Could be as soon as tonight though can't be 100% sure on that." He hit send.

Pete was playing chess with someone in Sri Lanka when the notification came through. Tentatively, he clicked the link to download it and readied himself to watch. From Jim's description he knew it wouldn't be easy viewing . When he got to the place that had upset Jim so much he could see why. There on the floor of the woods was a pile of around 10 dead dogs slung in a heap, though it was hard to make out that they were indeed dogs before they had been half torn apart. His stomach rolled and he carried on through the footage, hoping that was as bad as it got. His screen showed the outside of a big old barn, the view circling around once before going inside the barn. There were cages of heavy-set dogs down one side, the treadmills used for training them evident nearby. But it was the other smaller dogs in cages along the back wall that caught his interest. There in the middle one, all alone and looking frightened to death, was a dog that looked familiar – a little white Jack Russell terrier with a tan patch.

Chapter Twenty-Nine

PETE SAT STARING at the screen. This had never been part of the plan. A bit of harmless dognapping to get money was all it was supposed to be, a scam – nobody getting hurt. And up until now that had been it, a steady stream of income with little to do for it.

He looked back at his screen, the footage frozen on the little white Jack Russell, and there was no doubt about where he'd seen it before. The tell-tale tan patch over its left eye made it identifiable. One thing he did know about Jack Russells in particular was that no two had the same markings – there wasn't another terrier out there that looked like the one he was looking at now. It was definitely the one they'd had in the basement up until yesterday. The one that Vic had said wasn't safe to hand back. The one they'd already taken the ransom money for and undoubtedly the one Niles had done a deal for in the pub.

The question now was what should he do about it? He was involved in this new scam by default, though it wasn't what he'd signed up for, and there was no point having it out with Niles because he was sure to tell him to mind his own business. Niles knew full well Pete hadn't the balls to go to the cops. Anyone that has been in trouble with the law never went voluntarily, it would be tantamount to suicide.

He chewed on a fingernail thinking, letting his techie brain find a way to help without incriminating himself. He could make use of his knowledge to send the file to the right person and cover his tracks, couldn't he? He chewed some more. After 10 minutes he had the basis of a plan forming; he just needed to figure out some of the finer details, like who was the best contact at the police to work with. Any policeman worth his salt with a compassionate side that stood out should be active in their community, so he opened a browser window and typed in his search term, then waited for the page to load. There were plenty of results to choose from but he glanced at the first couple at the top of the page and clicked on one that spoke to him, The Daisy Chain. The page filled his screen and he smiled to himself because the name reminded him of his late mother: when he was little, he could remember his mother making daisy chains whenever they went for walks in the nearby fields, she wearing them for the rest of the day until they wilted. His father used to tease her for them saying she was way too old for such stupid things but she wasn't deterred. Fond memories of a woman gone.

Pete scrolled down to look at the posts and comments, and wasn't surprised to see several had put two and two together and knew pets simply weren't getting lost, they were being stolen. The locals knew all about the dognapping operation. It was the first time he'd ever really felt ashamed of what they did for a living. He read through the comments, many from those being affected themselves, with people wishing their beloved pets a speedy return, and even more comments from people wishing the gang death by a thousand cuts and various other ways to cause hurt. It made him feel sick to the stomach to be a part of it. Then he came across the picture of Jack, the dog that was still missing, the dog his group was responsible for and, if he didn't get a move on, the dog that would be almost certainly be dead very soon.

"Jack, hang in there, I'm going to try and help you."

He looked through the profile pictures and names of those that had commented, clicking through to read their profiles until he found what he was looking for. @Cagney.

"Now with a name like that you've got to be what I'm looking for," and he clicked through to read the profile. Amanda Lacey, occupation detective.

"Got you." He smiled at the reference to the old '80s American TV series *Cagney and Lacey*, something else his mother had loved. Mary Beth was her favourite character, a woman she'd admired because she was a strong working mother. He quickly created a fictitious profile, added a random image taken off the internet, and joined in the conversation.

From @PeterPan – "Who is working these cases @Cagney? I'm assuming the police are involved?"

He waited, hoping she would come back straight away, though why she'd be sitting looking at the site when she'd probably got other things to do he didn't know. Worth a try though. It wasn't Amanda that saw it first, but Ruth, and she responded straight away.

@PeterPan from McRuth – Hi PeterPan, DS Amanda Lacey, as you've assumed, is looking after it. Have you been a victim too?"

@McRuth – No, but I might have info. I'll contact her directly then."

Then he left as quickly as he'd arrived. He deleted the fake profile and closed the fictitious account before she or anyone else could respond. Now he had the right name, all he needed was her email address. When she saw the footage and had the GPS coordinates, she'd have to act quickly and he hoped all this wasn't going to be in vain. He opened another page and searched for the telephone number of the police station and asked the receptionist for Amanda's email address. So far so good. Now all he had to do was open up his Tor browser to keep things totally anonymous, create a fake email address, choose the file he wanted to link to and a few keystrokes later his work was complete. He hit send and imagined the message bouncing around the world via thousands of different relays to conceal his location, landing in DS Amanda Lacey's inbox sometime soon. He would be able to see when she'd clicked the link and hoped she'd see it quickly. Before sending it he had used the option to not close it down after the first download. He figured she'd want to show it to her colleagues and a vanishing URL after one view wouldn't be much use. If in the next 60 minutes she still hadn't seen it, he'd have to make an anonymous call, something he really didn't want to risk.

"It's now in motion, Jack."

Chapter Thirty

Amanda's working partner was Jack Rutherford, an older man that had spent many years as a Detective Constable and was happy with his lot. With no plans to be anything more than a great detective, he'd been working in the police for nearly 30 years, spending time in Oxford before he came to Croydon. He worked with surnames rather than first names for his colleagues because he felt that's where your character was, your roots. If he phoned you and you didn't answer, he'd leave his surname only and that was your cue to call 'Rutherford' back. No need for a message. It annoyed the hell out of everyone to ever experience it, but old dogs and new tricks and all that. ELO ran through his veins. 'Sweet Talkin' Woman' was his all time favourite, and one he'd often be heard humming while he worked. His wavy but thinning salt-and-pepper hair needed a good cut but without a woman at home to prod and take care of him, he never really got around to it. He missed his sweet-talkin woman every single day.

"About time you got a trim Jack, before The Boss tells you

again. Want me to get my scissors?" Amanda was teasing him and he didn't care. He was trying to figure out the new coffee machine that had been installed in their small break room. A plop plop shshsh could be heard and Amanda smiled, hoping he'd finally got the hang of it, though she wouldn't bet on it. She watched as he waited for his brew, his back turned towards her, and waited for the inevitable cursing outburst. It wasn't long.

"Shit, done it again!" She knew exactly what he'd done, or not done as it were.

"I wondered if you'd remember to put the damn pod in," she laughed. "For a detective, you can't half screw up the simple things, Jack."

"If you're so smart at making sodding coffee without a kettle and a jar of instant, why don't you make it, save my blood pressure!" She got up from her seat, scraping the chair back on the tiled floor as she did so.

"Shift out the way then, let the expert in." He glared at her and she mock glared back. "Look, it's simple. Put a pod here in this slot before you start. Then do what you've been doing. It's not hard." There was no bad will in her tone, just friendly banter, and Jack grunted in reply. The machine started up again, the plop plop shshsh this time bringing the aroma of fresh coffee with it, and no cursing. She handed him his mug with a smile.

"Now, tantrum over, can we get back to discussing the case?" At that moment her phone buzzed with a new email and she reached across the table to get it, not recognising the email address as she did so. Clicking the email open she saw a brief message and a link. It read:

"Reckon this is set for tonight, coordinates enclosed. Know you'll take care of it."

"Odd, looks like a tip-off about something."

"What is it, Lacey," he said as he went back for the sugar he'd forgotten.

"Not sure yet, hang on." She clicked the link to find out. A video filled her screen without sound and it took her a moment to realise what she was looking at.

"Jack, you'd better see this, looks like a pro fighting ring. There's a pile of torn dog corpses and footage of the building and dog cages. Looks like it's been captured via a drone." He was by her side in an instant.

"Hell, I reckon you're right," Jack said, looking over her shoulder at her phone screen, his attention fully engaged. "And judging by the barriers set up in a circle, and the dogs in those cages, it's sometime soon. Where is it, do you know?"

"Anonymous tip-off but they've given the coordinates, let's put them in and see where it is." She opened her web browser, punched in the details and waited for the destination to load.

"Some place out rural near Chatham. Wonder why they sent the link to me rather than Kent police?" She watched the video again then paused it. A little white and tan face looked back at her, telling her why in an instant.

"I think I know why. Look," she said, pointing to the screen. "See that little Jack Russell terrier in the back there? It's a missing local dog, saw it on The Daisy Chain two days ago."

"On the what?"

"Tell you about it later, but now, we need to get in touch with Kent and let them in on this. Looks like our local dognappers have found another line of business and this is where they're ending up."

"I'm on to it, forward that link to me and I'll get the ball rolling. In the meantime, we need to get some men out there to survey the place on the quiet, see what we can find out, see if it is tonight so we can bust them. And if it is tonight, the RSPCA need to notified, they'll want to take the dogs."

"Right, I'll organise this end and let the boss know, you liaise with Kent, and I'll see if I can find out who sent the email. We'll need to talk to them though I expect it's sent anonymous for a reason."

Chapter Thirty-One

"Right, looks like we're all set then." Tony was putting the final details together for the night's entertainment. "What time is the final text going out?"

"At 5pm. They know it's tonight, just not where exactly." Tony's sycophant Eddy was running the show with him as a learning experience. Tony was grooming him to take over the grunt work of organising so he didn't have to, just take his cut and keep out of trouble, and Eddy was a reasonably bright kid for a dumb shit. Still, he hadn't got to where he was without his many disposables, and Eddy was just one of them.

"Should be a good turnout tonight, if them from last month's fight bring a mate, should be about 50 of them, should be a good bit of cash changing hands, eh Ed?" He slapped the kid on his back in appreciation. "You done good on this one, let's see what the final total is tonight, might be a bonus in it for you." Ed smiled an excited grin to his boss at the prospect of a bonus, and thanked him.

"Great. Would appreciate that, Tony. Could get meself a dog like, really get into the fight scene like. Make some proper dough."

"Well, like I said, see what the final total is first. Now bugger off, I've got work to do," and strolled over to a large matt black Range Rover that was just pulling up outside the barn.

Eddy took the direct hint and went back to what he was doing, preparing the raw meat for the dogs who weren't doing any of the fighting tonight. Fighting dogs needed plenty of red meat to keep them mean and develop a taste for blood and it was part of his job as well as getting involved in their training, though tonight's fight dogs wouldn't be getting any. Being hungry and out for blood made them even more aggressive, and the angrier and more aggressive they got, the more the punters loved it. Another part of his job was to untie the dead bait animals that they tethered for the fight dogs to practice on, a part of the job he really didn't like. While he wasn't a soft touch, that bit always turned his stomach, but he supposed it was necessary. He glanced at the wheelbarrow with yesterday's dead in, ready to be dumped.

"Shit, I'd forgotten about them," he said to himself. "Bloody good job Tony ain't seen 'em," and threw an old nearby sack over them until he'd finished prepping the meat, vowing to do it next. Voices broke into his thoughts.

"Okay Mac, I'll see you in a few then, eh? Should be a good money night."

"Yeah Tony, but remember, my bets are all placed, I ain't betting in public view so don't try your tricks to get more from me, eh? I'm just an observer remember."

"Whatever Mac, I'll see ya later."

Mac left the building and climbed into his Range Rover that was parked just outside the big doors. He started the engine, putting his foot to the floor, spinning his wheels, shooting stones and dust behind as the tyres fought for traction. As MacAlister left the premises, Tony cleared his sinuses onto the dry dusty ground and walked back inside.

Chapter Thirty-Two

A SHORT DISTANCE AWAY, a camera fitted with a long-range lens captured the license plate of the vehicle as it left and fed it back to the station, though the policeman hiding in the bushes knew just who the vehicle belonged to, it was too distinctive. And that was the problem with private registration plates that were words not digits – they were easily remembered. He'd had dealings with the driver before. He was a slippery one, always seemed to have his bases covered, letting one of his men take the rap instead. He had loyalty as strong as the Mafia. He wondered what part MacAlister's role was in this operation but it didn't surprise him to see he was involved, it was just his type of shady shit.

Further back and behind the policeman in the woods was Jim, looking like he was just out for a stroll, Duke close by his side on his leash. He took his phone out of his pocket and sent a text to Pete:

"Good news. Looks like they've taken it seriously, men watching the building already." He clicked send and waited to see if there was a reply on its way back. The immediate vibration told him yes. It read:

"Great. Fingers crossed it ends tonight. Thinking of coming to watch the action."

Jim replied with: "I wouldn't bother, bit risky but up to you, I'll monitor anyway." He put his phone back in his pocket and made his way quietly out of the woods and back home.

Pete looked at his phone, trying to decide what to do. There was still plenty of time to get across to Chatham but would it do any good or was he putting himself in the wrong spot needlessly, in danger as Jim suggested? Something was drawing him to go and he knew it wasn't morbid interest; it wasn't the fights he wanted to see. As long as the police did their job and had followed up on his anonymous tip, all should be under control, but still something niggled at him, making him feel like he needed to do something. He looked around his dingy bedroom, the simple mattress on the floor in the corner, the old makeshift desk with his laptop on top, about the only thing of value in his life. That was something he had been thinking about a lot of late. He didn't particularly like the others much, Niles was a bully and Vic? Well, Vic just wanted to hang around Niles, something Niles could never see. They say three is a crowd, and he knew he wanted out, but how could he now, would Niles let him go? And doing what for a living exactly? Once upon a time he'd dreamt of being a mechanic, get a trade so he always had something to fall back on when he left school, but his dad's actions had put paid to that and he'd dropped out of school soon after. With no parents around to guide him and in his early teens, he'd rebelled, and that's how he'd found himself in juvie the first time. The second time? Well, he hadn't learned his lesson from the first time so it was just more of the same. Now he wished he'd done things differently and taken up the offer of help when the authorities had given it. But what foster family wanted a troubled teen lad? This was his life now, the route he'd chosen, but he wished it wasn't. He was just about to close his laptop down when he saw a now-familiar face looking back at him from the footage he'd been watching again and he knew what he was going to do.

Chapter Thirty-Three

IT WAS 6.30pm and cars and vans were making their way up the gravel track towards the makeshift ring that had been set up outside the big barn. A large circle of barriers lined with ply wood literally took centre stage and mainly men gathered in small groups, laughing and joking, introducing their mates to one another and generally revving up for the evening's entertainment. Cigarette smoke floated on air mixed with bad language and male hormones, the intense barking and yelping adding to the charged atmosphere. From their place high in a tree away from it all sat Pete and Jim, not daring to get any closer and not daring to watch via drone. They knew the police were up ahead watching and waiting and they were as close as they felt comfortable with.

"Shit Jim," Pete whispered, "how long are they going to leave it before they make their move? It's got to be nearly time!"

"Shhh Pete," Jim whispered back angrily. "Keep quiet and just watch, will you." Pete was a bag of nerves waiting and wished he'd stayed in his room and left them to it, it had been tricky enough to nip out as it was. He'd have some explaining to do when he got back. Niles would be pissed at him for sure for taking their only vehicle without asking.

He lifted the binoculars to his eyes and looked across at the big barn where the dogs were all ready. There were 12 obvious fighting dogs that all looked like they'd had an intense and heavy training life. Judging by the size of their necks, they had spent some considerable time strengthening hanging from tyres by their jaws. Even from his distance away the old scars on the dogs were evident, as were their clipped ears. Pete moved the lenses around further to the other paraphernalia that was visible. He could see the swim tank – something else used for training and muscle building – and the rotating wheel that the dogs chased live bait on to build stamina. It was a grotesque sight and he prayed it would all be stopped, that this illegal pastime would soon be busted wide open before another animal got badly hurt. How these spectators could think this was good old sport he'd never know.

He carried on scanning the cages along the back wall that were still filled with the small bait dogs. Their mouths had been taped shut. He hoped it was to keep the noise down, and not so they couldn't defend themselves, though in his heart he knew it was probably the latter. In the third cage along was a little trembling white face with a tan patch across his eye, looking terrified. It was Jack. Without saying a word, Pete mentally sent a message to the dog to hold on in there, he'd be safe soon. Pete turned his attention back to the yard and the makeshift ring where the referee, a heavy-set tattooed man, was taking bets on the first two dogs that would be fighting. He was laughing and jeering, with a stump of a cigarette hanging from the corner of his mouth. He looked as hard as nails, and someone even a strong confident man wouldn't want to get on the wrong side of. Pete counted 45 people gathered altogether, and he hadn't seen any more vehicles drive up the track for a few minutes so it must be close to starting. He looked at his watch. It was 7.15pm. His attention shifted quickly as a bell rang to get the spectators' attention. Everyone fell silent. The referee was about to start the first fight.

"Come on! What are they waiting for?" Pete said in an urgent whisper to Jim, who was also thinking the same thing. Surely they weren't going to let the first dogs start? They both watched in the distance as the first two dogs were brought out, each snarling and baring teeth to antagonise the other. Their half barks and yelps almost turned Pete's stomach, he couldn't face being this close if they were going to let them in the pit together, but he couldn't leave now either. He'd have to do his best to control himself.

Then all hell let loose.

Chapter Thirty-Four

FROM OUT OF nowhere it seemed, a heavy mob of police officers sprang into action and it was organised chaos. As Pete and Jim watched the mass of black uniforms surge forward in a large circle, people tried to flee on foot in all directions, some heading for their vehicles and what they hoped would be a quick escape, and some into the nearby woods, but they were outnumbered and rapidly apprehended. The two men that were each holding a fight dog tried to use them as weapons to keep from being arrested but the officers had come prepared and the dogs were soon temporarily restrained, allowing their handlers to be apprehended along with the rest of the onlookers. Jim spotted MacAlister slipping away towards the back of the barn, obviously hoping to get away unnoticed, it wouldn't do his reputation any good to be arrested, but it was too late. Focusing his lenses further out, he saw more police circling around behind the barn and it wasn't long before the big arrogant man was tussled to the ground and handcuffed like the rest.

The scene resembled a disturbed ant nest, black uniforms were running and gathering and returning with prisoners back to their vans, which had now been driven in closer and were filling up fast with men shouting obscenities. Not far behind them were the animal rescue vans, RSPCA clearly visible written down the side. If the dogs inside the barn only knew what those particular vans represented, they would have sighed a collective sigh of relief at the prospect of being set free from their hell. Pete and Jim stayed put high up in their vantage point, not daring to move until everyone below had been rounded up and were safely imprisoned in a police wagon. But it was the dogs that were concerning Pete, were they all okay, and in particular, was little Jack okay? He strained his eyes to see what was happening but with so much activity and the fading light it was near impossible.

He counted six animal rescue vans. Quite clearly they hadn't known exactly what they would be dealing with. Heavily protected animal rescue staff were waiting for the go-ahead to move in and get to work. As fully loaded police wagons edged their way back down the gravel track, rocking slightly from side to side as they went, the activity slowed from the previous chaotic pace to a more manageable investigation level and both Pete and Jim finally felt a sense of relief. There were just the animals to take care of now, and then the police could catalogue their findings. He knew from what he'd seen himself, there was plenty of evidence of an organised and professional ring, and the two of them had managed to bust it wide open. Pete turned to Jim with his palm in the air and high fived him heartily, giving a loud cheer as he did so, forgetting the fact they were still hiding in the tree. They'd been so focused on what was happening in the distance, they hadn't noticed the police officers below them checking for absconders, and now their cover was blown. As an officer called up to them to both come down, all Pete could think of was that he was in for another stint inside, only now it would be far worse than juvie.

Chapter Thirty-Five

AMANDA TOOK in the sight with bewilderment. She'd seen some bad shit in her time but nothing had prepared her for something so grotesque it was barely imaginable. But the human race would never cease to surprise her with what they were capable of. She turned to Jack Rutherford, seeing a look of bewilderment on his face too. Even though he'd spent a good few years more in the force than Amanda, it didn't make his stomach any stronger, only his resolve.

"Holy hell."

"Holy hell alright, this must be one of the biggest, most organised we've ever come across. Usually it's a few blokes in a garage or a field some place with a couple of dogs, nothing like this operation." Jack was incredulous as he took in the scene around him. The spectators and organisers had been captured and were now travelling in the back of police trucks to be processed. The only people now present were the scene technicians, a handful of uniformed officers and the RSPCA, who were still busy checking the animals, having had to first wait for the scene guys to photograph their findings. As there were no dogs apparently in immediate stress, they'd had to sit tight and wait, otherwise convictions could have been at stake. Nobody wanted the culprits to fall through a stupid loophole. Amanda pointed at some of the equipment – some she could guess what it was used for, but not others.

"I can guess the treadmills are used for exercising the dogs on, for hours at a time I expect, but what is that circular one for?" Jack unfortunately knew the answer, as it was not his first dog-fighting ring gig.

"See that post next to it? That's where they tie the fight dog and then antagonise it with live bait, usually a small dog or a cat even, then when the dog's wound up enough, they let it have the bait as a reward. All part of its training. Sick bastards."

Amanda had to agree with that. The chains and pulleys, packs of protein powder, breaking sticks to separate fighting dogs, thick weights on chains, and the swim tank were all evidence of a sick and rather grand enterprise that probably supplied other sick operators all over the country, possibly even Ireland and beyond. It was big business, though the trick was to keep it as secret and exclusive as possible. And they had until now.

"Who would want to come and be entertained by this kind of thing, Jack? Who in their right mind?" Amanda was still struggling with what she was seeing.

"Well, it's not all your working class as you might expect. Big money changes hands at these events, and the average Joe in the street doesn't have that kind of dough lying around. Tends to be those a bit better off, or those with a gambling problem."

"That surprises me. You see rough-looking youths in the street with pit bulls, I'd just assumed it was the likes of them."

"Afraid not, they're just the 'chain rollers', the ones that get together in parks or their street usually, and set their dogs at each other for fun and status, but the dogs are on chains rather than let loose. Still damn cruel and the dogs will often lose an ear or an eye. But it's status, see? Who wants to mess with someone that has the strongest most vicious dog on the street with them? No, this is the big time stuff," he said, waving his arm around at what was around them both.

Amanda slowly walked further into the old barn. What a dump. The old wooden sidings of the building let long thin strips of dying light in, like dim strip lights placed vertically instead of horizontally, and that meant the place was probably wet and drafty in colder weather. She felt for the dogs' misery at being held captive in this place as well as their purpose in life. She walked along further to the cages that still contained some of the animals, the RSPCA now able to remove some and treat them. She looked at the small metal confines a large pit bull had been kept in, its faeces evident in the back, its water bowl contaminated, and no evidence of any food. Her stomach rolled, and not for the first time tonight. There must have been 20 of the same style of cages, but there were only a dozen or so fighting dogs evident. That probably meant others had once lived here, if you could call it living, and had either died or been transferred out further afield. The even smaller cages along the back wall took her attention and she approached slowly, still finding it hard to take in the sights and putrid smell. An RSPCA woman was examining a little Bichon Frise that was trembling beyond belief. It had parcel tape around its mouth that the officer was gently trying to remove.

"Can I give you a hand," Amanda enquired, not wanting the little thing to suffer any more.

"It's fine thanks, nearly done getting it off. Just make sure the lowlife that does this type of thing gets sent down, would you? Makes me so god damn mad!"

The anger in her voice startled Amanda for a moment,

but she guessed she also never got accustomed to the findings her work brought her each day either. This whole sorry building was full of terror and upset, humans and dogs both included. Then she saw the Jack Russell terrier, he too with his mouth taped closed, and went over to his cage.

The female officer she'd just been talking to approached her. "Sorry about my little outburst just then. It's not your fault, but these scumbags will hardly get the gavel rapped at them never mind a decent sentence and it makes my blood boil."

"You don't need to apologise, I feel the same way, I think we all do," she said, trying to smile in comfort for both of them. "See this little dog?' she said, pointing into his cage. "He's called Jack, and he's missing from nearby to me. Do you think when he's been checked out, I could take him back with me? I'm sure his owners would be delighted to get him back tonight if he's okay to go."

"Well, it's a bit irregular, but I'll double-check with my boss and see. Not my decision to make, I'm sure you understand."

Amanda nodded her agreement and smiled at the woman, then turned her attention back to little Jack at the back of his small cage. "Not long now, buddy, soon have you back home where you belong, just a little while longer." Amanda then moved to one side as the animal officer opened his cage to start her examination. The other Jack was calling her name from the other side of the building so she headed over. He was half hanging outside what appeared to be an internal door leading to the office of the operation. She followed him inside.

"There's no doubt about this being a big operation," he said, pointing to what looked like a ledger. "Look at this, must be old school, they never heard of digital files to keep shit like this? It's a bit less obvious and a damn site easier to hide than an old book, silly sods."

"Well, I guess you don't have to be bright to be a scumbag criminal like this lot. Just makes it easier for us. What else have you found?" Amanda knew there had to be more. He pulled out the bottom drawer of an ancient, once-grey metal filing cabinet, and beckoned her to look.

"Shit, how much is in there?"

"Don't know exactly but I'd say maybe a couple of hundred thousand, give or take. And that's not from tonight's bets because we busted them before it took off. Obviously never heard of a safe either, dumb asses. I tell you, thick as pig shit this lot."

"I wonder how long they've been in operation. Any idea from that ledger?"

"Well, that one starts back in 2004 so at least 12 years. Who knows if there's an older ledger somewhere. They'd have made a mint during that time."

"I saw MacAlister being taken away, his face was pure fury. A bit far off the beaten track for him, isn't it? I always knew he was into bigger things than his betting shop, I'm guessing now that's just a front. Slippery sod."

"Yeah, I saw him too, but he wasn't half as angry as that big tattooed guy, Tony something or other. He's the main operator. I think you'll find MacAlister was just a small part, a way for him to get money without too much dirt on his hands."

"That figures. Anyhow, when we're all done here, I've asked to take one of the little dogs back with me, he's missing locally and I'm sure he'd like to get back home as soon as possible." Amanda smiled at him before adding, "You'd like him, he's called Jack actually." And for the first time that evening, Jack smiled back.

Chapter Thirty-Six

LIONEL ENTERED the living room of his small terraced house, a tray in his hands, a Rogan Josh on board, and sat down in his rather old fashioned Draylon chair to watch the late news with his supper. Making himself comfortable, he flicked to the right channel with the remote, chewed on a fork full of curry and waited for the program to start. Moments later the familiar music played and the headlines were read out, making his fork pause on its way to his open mouth. He couldn't believe what he was hearing as the reporter started on the main story.

"What the..."

There on the screen was footage of the police at an old barn somewhere, the headlines stating a dog-fighting ring had been busted and locals had been arrested. While the report wasn't showing any footage of who those locals were, there was footage of the location, somewhere near Chatham in Kent. As the cameras had arrived after the main raid, there wasn't much they were able to film, and the police kept the reporters behind the restricted area of the scene, but one thing had got caught in their camera lens – a distinctive matt black Range Rover with dark windows was parked under a tree in the makeshift car park, along with other cars. Lionel barely heard what the reporter on the scene was saying but from the footage in front of him, he knew what had gone down.

"I bloody knew he was involved in some big shit, and I hope they throw the book at him!" Putting his tray down on the coffee table in front of him, he turned the volume up to listen to more about what had gone on. The cameras panned back to show the extent of the area, the RSPCA and police still sorting through what was left behind. The reporter hadn't got much to say except the raid was thought to be one of the biggest in UK history and arrests were expected to be made. The newsreader moved on to something more mundane, so he picked his tray back up and tried to finish his supper, though his appetite had gone.

Across town, others were also watching the same report, though they didn't yet know the half of it. It was only Ruth and a few others that knew that the spate of dognapping had then progressed to supplying live bait for a fighting ring, and as the report had played on, Ruth had noticed the unmistakable short cropped blond hair of Detective Amanda Lacey in amongst the mayhem. She was carrying a little Jack Russell terrier in her arms that had been rescued. She live paused the picture and studied it for a moment, smiling at both Amanda and the dog that she instantly recognised as the missing little Jack.

Chapter Thirty-Seven

"Look, I'm telling you, I wasn't there to watch the fight, I was there to watch the raid. That's why I was sat in a tree!" Pete was being interrogated by the Kent police and he was getting worried he could be in big trouble. His frustration was coming out in his words. The detective carried on his questioning.

"And how did you know about a raid then, in order to be up that tree in the first place?"

"Because I was the one who notified the police, like I've already told you half a dozen times but you don't seem to want to hear that." Pete tried to calm himself a little, his anguish evident, but he didn't want to get on the wrong side of this detective. He tried again, this time a bit calmer. "Look, you've probably already discovered I've a juvie record and that's why I'm keen to keep out of trouble, and why I sent an anonymous tip-off rather than expose myself. Ask the detective I sent it to if you don't believe me." Pete rested his head in his hands on the cheap table in the interview room, tired and worried. It had been a long night and right now he wished he'd stayed at home like Jim had suggested.

"And who would that be, because it wasn't anyone from this station."

"It was my local one, Croydon, her name is Lacey, DS Amanda Lacey. Please, double-check with her, I sent her a link via an email, she'll verify it."

The detective made a note of the name and excused himself to check it out, leaving Pete sitting there on his own, with another policeman guarding the door. Pete rubbed his face and tried to keep calm. What could they get him on? Trespassing? Dognapping? Illegal drone-flying? In theory if they did their jobs well, all three, and probably something else he hadn't thought of. There was no way he was going back inside so he'd look after himself this time, and that could mean cutting a deal. He pondered on that thought as the detective came back in the room. He looked pissed at him.

"Seems you're telling the truth," he said. "She's confirmed your story, though there are some questions she'd like to ask you yourself. And I still have some of my own too. Like how did you get that footage in the first place?" Pete knew how this was now going to end up.

"I'm not saying another word to you. Either charge me or let me go." He sat back with his arms folded, his body language telling the detective the questioning had probably come to an end.

"Look lad, we have enough to charge you and hold you on, it's just how much more we add to those charges, so don't get cocky with me. This isn't *CSI*, it's real life and you're in the shit." He looked at his watch, it was after 11pm. "But it will wait until the morning now so I suggest you make yourself comfortable in your cell for the night, and we'll take this back up again in the morning."

"Then I want to speak to DS Lacey, and I want a lawyer and I'm not saying another word until I have them both."

THE CONTROLLER

Pete knew he needed to use his tip-off to help him and Jim out of this mess, and he hoped Detective Lacy would be a bit more sympathetic. He stood and was escorted back to his cell for the night, where he lay awake thinking of the best approach to get himself and Jim out of the mess he'd put them both in. There was only one way to do it that he could see.

Chapter Thirty-Eight

AMANDA DROVE BACK from the Kent police station mid-morning after spending time interviewing Pete and coming to an agreement that both he and his lawyer were happy with. To his credit, he wasn't like all the other scumbags she dealt with, he seemed quite a gentle soul. Having looked into his background, she saw that he'd just been one of those that had fallen through the cracks of life and had ended up fending for himself from prematurely early on. While that hardened a lot of individuals, for some it simply made life a struggle, succumbing to bullies like Niles who took advantage. They'd managed to come to a deal. He'd be done for illegally flying his drone and trespassing but not for the dognapping. He'd given up the identities of Niles and Vic and they'd been given an early awakening and arrested and charged early this morning, so he was off the hook there. Without his tip-off, they'd never have caught the ringleaders in the dog-fighting raid, resulting in criminal charges being brought against eight men as they had fought to save their own skins and deal. Shame they hadn't thought about saving the skins of the dogs they'd abused. The law urgently needed reviewing in her mind, they'd get pittance sentences. Even on several offences, they'd only serve a handful of years and they knew it, but the police could only work within the lines of the law, they didn't make the rules. And little Jack was safely back with his owners, who had understandably been delighted to have him returned fit and well, though a bit shaken up. She flicked her indicator to turn into Richmond Road and pulled up outside Ruth's place. She'd called earlier to double-check she was there and not at her office, and Ruth was waiting for her.

"Come in," Ruth greeted her on the front step. "Can I get you a coffee? If you don't mind me saying, you look like you could do with one." Always the direct one.

Amanda looked at her as she entered the hallway and followed her down to the kitchen at the back of the house. "That bad eh?"

"I saw it on the TV last night. I'm guessing you've been a bit busy all night?"

"You guessed right there. I've just left the Kent police and the individual that sent us the tip-off. It's been a full-on few hours." Ruth pointed to a chair and Amanda flopped into it. It felt the most natural thing in the world to do in what was virtually a stranger's house. It wasn't lost on Ruth, this woman just seemed to fit right in. Ruth put a capsule in the machine and waited for the familiar plop plop to start.

"I'm guessing you haven't eaten much either, want some toast, or a sandwich perhaps?" While Amanda really wanted to take her up on the offer of food, it wasn't the done thing. She opened her mouth to respond no but Ruth took charge before she could voice her reply.

""I'll put you two slices in and there's more if you want it," then took butter and marmalade out of the cupboard and put them on the little table in front of her. Amanda didn't try to refuse.

"Thanks, that's lovely of you," Amanda said wearily, and

gave Ruth a quick smile, watching her make the second cup of coffee, the plop plop starting all over again. With her back to Amanda, Ruth asked, "So what happens now then? The ringleaders have been arrested I'm guessing, the dogs examined and rehomed, then what? How did you find out about the ring?

"Well, to answer your first question, they'll appear in court and hopefully end up in prison, but that's some time away unfortunately, so they'll probably be back out on the street tomorrow. The dogs may never be rehomed, they may have to be put to sleep depending on whether they can be retrained enough to live a normal dog's life, but the RSPCA will work hard with them and decide what needs to be done for the best. And to answer your last question, we got an anonymous tip-off, from the lad that actually found the dognapping targets with his drone as it turns out. He sent us a TOR link to the location footage beforehand. He was part of a small gang of three, the local dognappers that were working the town, but when the leader, a man named Niles, got approached to sell the dogs on to the fight ring for bait, he didn't want to be a part of it. Seems his drone buddy Jim accidentally found the venue while trespassing one day and they put two and two together and did something about it."

Ruth sat down with her own coffee, having put two slices of toast on a plate for Amanda. They sat silently for a moment, just the scraping sound of butter being spread atop crunchy toast by Amanda.

"What is the young lad like? He's obviously got a conscience, and is clever, not many people are aware of TOR and what it can be used for." Ruth stared into her coffee thoughtfully.

"He's had his share of bad luck, a rough childhood, a stint in juvie, but he seems different than the others we come across. And without his conscience and sending that link, we'd be none the wiser to what was going on. He saved a lot of pain at last night's event."

"And his fate?"

"He's cut a deal, so he'll be fine. He'll probably get community service for aviation violations or some such, but he's off the hook for dognapping. He's given us the brains of the gang so we're happy." She took a large bite of marmaldey toast and tried to speak, then gave up. Ruth watched with amusement.

"I meant to say," Amanda tried again, "why the interest in him?"

"Ah, you know. Always on the lookout for bright techies, it's my business. Maybe when this dies down, I could meet him, maybe give him some work to occupy his mind, keep him out of trouble. He sounds bright, just needs a better direction."

Amanda liked the idea of that. Something had made her feel differently about this lad and if Ruth was happy to at least meet with him, maybe she could put the two together and do some good. She drank back the last of her coffee and buttered the remaining piece of toast.

"More coffee?" Ruth asked hopefully.

"That would be lovely," Amanda said, her eyes meeting Ruth's.

Read on to go back in time ....

Hey You, Pretty Face.

Chapter 1

SUNDAY 19TH DECEMBER, 1999. Almost Christmas.

It was going to hurt. She knew it would hurt far more than the act of giving birth itself had done, not an hour ago. But life for the little one would be so much better without her, with someone else who could take care of her, give her everything she would ever want for, a life the young woman hadn't a chance to offer her.

"Goodbye, little one. I'm doing this because I love you, not because I don't want you. It'll be better for you this way."

She kissed her baby's forehead before wrapping her tightly in the swaddle she had. The infant whimpered a little. Perhaps she was trying to communicate, asking her not to go. Perhaps they could find a way to be together; it wouldn't be that bad. But the woman knew it could never be anything else, and as tough as it was, she knew she had to stick to her decision. Inside her, two voices screamed loudly at each other, straining her chest: one urging her to leave her child, the other sobbing, pleading with her not to go through with it.

Deep down, she knew there was no choice and, mumbling

words of comfort to herself, she tried to quiet the voice begging her to stop. With the whimpering child wrapped in a towel and tucked inside her only coat, she placed the tiny bundle inside the porch of the church doorway, tucked away from the relentless biting wind and sleet that was beginning to fall. With the baby safe for now and out of harm's way, she was sure she would be secure for the night. Someone would surely open the church door in the morning and take her in. The child's life from that moment on would be so much better than the alternative. She shivered and hugged her arms. She knew she would be cold without her coat, but the little one needed it more. It was the least she could do, her last solo act of kindness for her daughter before she walked away.

Forever.

The young woman barely felt the wetness falling on her shoulders as she disappeared back into the street and the darkness, the hot tears streaming down her face cooling quickly as they fell away. She rubbed her arms, more out of needy emotion and comfort than anything else. The sleet melted on contact with her thin sweatshirt, soaking the fabric. Even though she was shivering, she didn't notice the vibrations shaking her body. Her only focus was the sheer desperation of the situation, the intense hopelessness that was her short life so far. At least her baby wouldn't have to be part of it now, would have a fighting chance with someone else, someone more able, someone less useless, someone less scarred.

Someone a million times better than she was.

Inside the church, an older woman sat praying quietly, grieving for how her life had turned out so far but without tears. It was a comfort to her to simply sit here in the dim light, praying in silence, though she'd never bothered with the church before she'd gone away. No time for it, she'd always said. Not relevant to her. No interest in hocus-pocus. How the tables had turned and times had changed since she'd returned to Croydon only four weeks ago.

Prison changed you, for one thing, and it did so particularly if you were the victim of continual abuse as she had been. Day after day, night after night they'd come for her both mentally and physically. The prison guards had turned blind eyes to her suffering, monitoring her from a distance until things went as far as the guards dared them to and then stepping in at the last minute. Even the infirmary hadn't been a safe haven.

But then, paedophiles deserved what they got, apparently. More so the female ones. The other prisoners couldn't comprehend what went on in her head to have committed such an abhorrent crime. It was far worse than murder, in their opinions, and her punishment should be that much harsher. She'd cried like her victims had, willing her death to come.

Oh, how she'd prayed, but those prayers had gone unanswered. But she was free again now.

Gathering her few belongings and wrapping her flimsy scarf around her head, ready for the icy wind outside, she made her way to the front door and steeled herself for the walk back to the halfway house she'd been placed in. It wasn't far, but in mid-winter, and in this weather, it would be far enough on foot. The valuable little money in her pocket was better spent on food than bus fare. Opening the heavy wooden door, she shuffled out into the porch and pulled her scarf a little tighter before descending the few steps, holding tightly to the handrail as she went. But halfway down, the woman stopped. Had she heard something over the howl of the wind? She stood still, straining to listen in the quiet street. On a night like this and so close to Christmas, sensible people were huddled away in their houses, more likely their beds at this late hour; there was not a soul outside but her.

Yes, there it was again – a sort of gurgle. The longer she stood listening, the more it gained strength. Was it coming from above her, where she'd come from? As she made her way carefully back up the steps, the sound became louder, more insistent, then developed into something she recognized, something acutely familiar. There was no doubt what it was.

The cry of a baby.

Chapter 2

THE JOLLY CARTER, shortened to The Jolly by the locals, was much the same as any backstreet public house around Croydon, or in fact in any other part of the country. A foggy haze of cigarette smoke hovered overhead with nowhere to go, as more and more rose from the mouths and noses of drinking customers. Whether you smoked or not, you ended up smoking by default. There was no choice, unless you wore an oxygen mask – although that would have given you added protection from the smell of urine as you passed the gents toilets. The gaudy décor of the establishment had, over the years, been covered with a thick veil of caramel nicotine that ran in streaks down the walls.

Workingmen – and they were mainly men – propped the bar up, some with a newspaper, others holding court and regaling the others with tales, each one better than the last. Some stood alone, searching for answers at the bottom of their pint pots. Tom Jones was "Burnin' Down the House" on a jukebox. It was Sunday lunchtime.

"Another when you're ready, please, Jim," Jack ordered, waving his empty glass in the barman's direction and catching his eye. The red-faced landlord nodded and made his way over to grab the glass.

"You're not going to be late for your lunch, are you, Jack? Your missus will be mad as hell..." He let the words dangle knowingly but Jack shook his head.

"I've time for one more, then I'll be off. A nice bit of roast beef, all the trimmings, a glass of wine maybe, and my old chair to sleep it off. What more could a man ever want for?" Jack grinned his contentment at his day ahead, but Jim was already retreating to the bitter pump to refill his glass. Jack watched the creamy head of ale come back his way a moment later and handed over a fistful of change.

"I wish I had someone upstairs to make my dinner and let me have a nice sleep after it."

"Then you need to get yourself a good woman, like my Janine," Jack said, taking a long mouthful and wiping the froth from his upper lip. "She's a good woman, that's for sure, though she'd give me hell if she could hear me telling you to find yourself a good woman. She'd tell you to get organized and do it yourself, stop being a lazy arse. And she'd be right."

"I ain't got time to peel spuds and shop for beef. I'm here all the time. Another reason I haven't got a woman – not many come in here, and those that do only come in to drag their husbands back home."

There wasn't much more Jack could add to that. He nodded his understanding and resignation to the landlord's retreating back as he made his way further down the bar to serve someone else. Jack studied his own pint for a moment, then was interrupted by the ringing of his mobile in his jacket pocket.

"That'll be Janine now, I'll bet. Right on time," he mumbled affectionately to himself. He flipped the top of the phone and answered it. It wasn't Janine. She wasn't calling him home for his Sunday lunch and an afternoon nap.

"DC Jack Rutherford. Hello."

"Jack, I need you to get yourself over to the hospital." It was the desk sergeant back at the station.

"What's up, Doug?"

"A newborn baby was handed in at the hospital not long ago. Seems the little one had been found abandoned in a church doorway. Someone dropped it off and must have left almost immediately after. As did the woman who handed the baby in. We need to track her down and find out who the baby belongs to. It's lucky to be alive if it spent the night out in the cold. Last night could have been the coldest one this winter. Could have frozen the balls off a brass monkey."

Jack looked at the remaining half of his glass of bitter as the sergeant went on, all visions of his Sunday roast fading away, not to mention his nap. And Janine wouldn't be too pleased, either.

"Any idea who the woman was and why she left so soon?"

"Nope and nope." Useful.

"Right. Best I get on my way, then."

The sergeant gave him the details of who to contact at the hospital and hung up. Jack took a last gulp of the remaining half and left the rest on the side, signalling to the barman he was off with a quick wave of his hand.

"Save me some, eh?" Jim called across in hope.

"I'll be lucky if I get any now. Been called into work."

Jim gave him a look that said "tough luck," and carried on wiping the bar with a damp cloth the colour of slate rooftop tiles. Jack hoped he didn't wash glasses with the same dirty cloth.

Heading towards the door and the cold midday air outside, he paused for a moment. He'd better give Janine a call and tell her he wouldn't make lunch. He pulled out his phone and pressed dial.

"Sorry, love. I've been called in. A baby has been found so I've got to go. Will you keep mine warm?"

"Oh, Jack! I was looking forward to a movie with you after lunch, too." She sounded disappointed. He hated doing that to her, but it couldn't be helped. As a detective's wife, she was used to it.

"I know, love. I'll be as quick as I can. You go ahead and eat. I'll have mine later. Then we'll watch the movie."

They said their goodbyes, Jack knowing full well that whatever happened between now and bedtime, he'd never see the movie past the opening credits.

Still, he'd be back home on the sofa with his Janine, and that was enough for him.

Chapter 3

IT WAS a good job he'd only had a pint and three quarters. A DUI for a detective never sat well with the public – or his boss, for that matter. Still, it wasn't a problem now, though Jack could have done with a sandwich to soak up the beer that was sloshing around his empty stomach. Janine had got him watching his weight, and so the Sunday breakfast routine they'd shared for as many years as he could remember had gone south. With her hands on her hips like an old ward matron she'd told him if Sunday lunch was to stay in place, he couldn't have both that and his afternoon pint. The thought amused him as he locked his car door and headed to the hospital's main entrance in search of Monica Johnson, the matron who had called the police.

The front entrance doors slid open automatically as he neared the sensor and he stepped inside; the bland pale greenish-blue décor and the smell of cleaning fluid were the same as most hospitals he'd ever been inside. Even on a Sunday, doctors, nurses and orderlies moved briskly about, some headed home, some on their break and some headed to the next part of their working day. They all minded their own business as they went, with no conversation between them, so Jack fell in behind a man wearing surgical scrubs, joined the human train and followed the signs to the special care baby unit where the infant was being cared for.

The baby. Who would abandon their child, and on such a cold night? Who would be so desperate or stupid to hope someone came for it before it was too late? Why not take it directly to the hospital straight off, or the police? But Jack already knew the answers: because she was scared. And this case would be no different.

Of what, though?

And ditto for the woman that had found the child – why not call an ambulance and the police straight away when she'd found it?

The sign for the SCBU was up ahead and he pushed the buzzer for admittance, his warrant card ready and visible through the glass partition. He waited, then he saw her. He instinctively knew it was her: Monica, authority written across her ample chest as she walked towards him. She reminded him of Hattie Jacques from a *Carry On* movie.

He chanced a smile. As she opened the door, she returned a flicker of one, though it vanished in an instant. Her name badge did indeed confirm she was Monica Johnson. And in charge.

"Good afternoon," Jack said politely, keeping his voice low. The ambience of the ward told him loud noise was not acceptable, and he was aware that his shoes sounded like the quick slaps of an elastic band on the lino as he followed her back towards her desk. He tried, and failed, to walk on the tips of his toes.

"Take a seat," Monica instructed, waving her hand to a spare chair. Glad to stop the sound of his own shoes, he sat, fiddling to get his notebook from his inside pocket. She sat opposite him, waiting.

"Why don't you start from the top and tell me everything you know? Then I'll ask a few questions." He beamed a reassuring smile and received another flicker in return.

"I'd only been on duty a few minutes, so it was not long after seven this morning. There was a phone call from the main entrance reception. The security guard called up saying a woman with a bundle needed help. She'd found a baby abandoned. Naturally, I went down to meet her and took a nurse with me, but when we'd got there, she was nowhere to be seen. The guard was holding the baby. I asked him what had happened, and he said the woman had found the baby last night about 11 pm at St George's church. She'd kept it warm until this morning, but it was hungry. Then she left without giving any more details. Another staff member went after her, but she wouldn't say another word apparently, so they gave up. All we can tell you is that she was about retirement age, grey-haired, and dressed a bit oddly, like from a charity shop perhaps. We've no idea where she comes from or her name." She sighed and ran a hand through her hair. "I wish I could tell you more."

"Has security checked the camera footage? I assume you have footage of the main desk and the outside of the building?"

"Yes. I have a copy for you, not that it shows much. She was alone and on foot, and had a scarf around her head and neck, to keep the cold out, I expect." She handed Jack a CD copy of the front desk and immediate outdoor camera footage.

"I may need to see more footage from further out. Who do I need to contact to get it?"

Monica wrote down the name and telephone number of the head of security and handed him the piece of paper.

"And how is the little one now? I hear it's a little girl."

"Doing well, considering her rough start. She was hungry,

but no hyperthermia or else I don't think she'd be still with us. Last night was a particularly cold one, so she was lucky the lady found her. I wish she'd brought her straight here, though."

"Any sign of the mother? I'm guessing she gave birth elsewhere and you haven't seen her?"

"Correct. Everyone is accounted for on the maternity ward and in here, so I'd guess you are right, though she may need help herself. I suspect she gave birth in secret and on her own. She must be scared, confused maybe, and in need of medical attention."

"We'll keep an eye out, and we'll also check other hospitals and clinics nearby in case anyone has shown up needing help. Can you remember anything else, no matter how trivial you may think it is?" Jack was hoping for something he could use, big or small. He'd take small over nothing.

"The guard said the woman who dropped the baby off was extremely nervous herself, as though she couldn't stand to be in the hospital – frightened, maybe, though I don't know why she would be. Then she was gone without another word. It doesn't make any sense. Perhaps she had a bad experience in the past."

Jack wasn't convinced. "Maybe it wasn't the hospital that she was scared of. Maybe it was the camera she didn't like."

Click here to read the rest of the story.

Also by Linda Coles

Hot To Kill - Book 2 in the Amanda Lacey series

She's literally getting away with murder...

Madeline Simpson is hot, sticky, and stressed to the max. She's had it up to here with people treating her like dirt, and the hot flashes certainly aren't helping. When her temper causes her to accidentally murder her landscaper, she expects to live out the rest of her menopause in prison. But the police have their hands full with a series of sexual assaults...

Feeling above the law, Madeline aims to teach her biggest offenders a lesson. While her pranks take a dark and dangerous turn, Madeline begins to suspect the true identity of the serial sex offender.

To catch the culprit, Madeline will have to go it alone... or risk unburying her deadly secrets.

Also by Linda Coles

The Hunted - Book 3 in the AMANDA LACEY series

They kill wild animals for sport. She's about to return the favour...

Philippa is fed up with the big-game hunter posts clogging up her newsfeed. The passionate veterinarian can no longer sit back and do nothing when hunters brag about the exotic animals they've murdered and the followers they've gained along the way...

To stop the killings, Philippa creates her own endangered list of hunters. By stalking their profiles and infiltrating their inner circles, she vows to take them out one-by-one...

There's no telling how far Philippa will go to add the guilty to her own trophy collection. And she won't stop until their kind is extinct...

The Hunted is a suspenseful mystery set in the Detective Amanda Lacey series. If you like eclectic characters, untamed adventures, and revenge stories fit for the technological age, then you'll love this thrilling tale.

Also by Linda Coles

Dark Service - Book 4 in the AMANDA LACEY series

The dark web can satisfy any perversion, but two detectives might just pull the plug...

Taylor never felt the blade pressed to her scalp. She wakes frightened and alone in an unfamiliar hotel room with a shaved head and a warning... tell no one.

As detectives Amanda Lacey and Jack Rutherford investigate, they venture deep into the fetish-fueled underbelly of the dark web. The traumatised woman is only the latest victim in a decade-long string of disturbing—and intensely personal—thefts.

To take down a perverted black market, they'll go undercover. But just when justice seems within reach, an unexpected intruder sends their sting operation spiralling out of control. Their only chance at catching the culprits lies with a local reporter... and a sex scandal that could ruin them all.

Dark Service is the skin-crawling fourth novel in the Detective Amanda Lacey mystery series. If you like sexual intrigue, modern-day suspense, and exploring technology's dark side, then you'll love this cutting edge thriller from international bestselling author Linda Coles.

Buy *Dark Service* to lose yourself in the darkest corners of your imagination today.

Also by Linda Coles

One Last Hit - Book 5 in the AMANDA LACEY series

A tough detective. A family on the rocks. The greatest danger may come from inside his own house...

Detective Sergeant Duncan Riley has always worked hard to maintain order on the streets of Manchester. But when a series of incidents at home cause him to worry about his wife's behaviour, he finds himself pulled in too many directions at once. After a colleague Amanda Lacey asks for his help with a prescription drug epidemic, he never expected the case would infiltrate his own family...

As Riley and Lacey trace the drugs to a dangerous prepaid app, a scary situation with Riley's children takes his marriage to the breaking point. Little does he know that his home and work lives are about to collide, and the detectives may not survive the aftermath.

One Last Hit is a standalone novel in the gritty DS Amanda Lacey contemporary suspense series. If you like riveting drama, close-to-home crimes, and cops on the trail of justice, then you'll love Linda Coles' street-smart thrill-ride.

Buy One Last Hit to solve a crime with its finger on the pulse today!

About the Author

Hi, I'm Linda Coles. Thanks for choosing this book, I really hope you enjoyed it and collect the following ones in the series. Great characters make a great read and I hope I've managed to create that for you.

Originally from the UK, I now live and work in beautiful New Zealand along with my hubby, 2 cats and 7 goats. My office sits by the edge of my vegetable garden, my very favourite authors are Harlan Coben and Karin Slaughter and apart from reading and writing, I get to run by the beach for pleasure.

If you find a moment, please do write an honest online review, they really do make such a difference to those choosing what book to buy next.

Enjoy! And tell your friends.

Thanks, Linda

Keep in touch:
lindacoles.com
linda@lindacoles.com

Afterword

I hope you've enjoyed this, the first story for detectives Jack Rutherford and Amanda Lacey. There are plenty more stories to come in the series.

If you'd like to keep in touch with monthly news from myself about new books coming out or special offers, here's the link to my website to register. I promise you won't get any spam from me!

Thanks for reading this far.
  Linda

Printed in Poland
by Amazon Fulfillment
Poland Sp. z o.o., Wrocław